SOMEONE IN THE HOUSE

A door slammed.

"Who's there? Dad? Are you home?"

No answer.

The sound had come from upstairs. Maybe he had come home and hadn't heard her. But his car wasn't in the driveway. Who else would be in the house? Who else?

Who knew she'd be here alone?

The door slammed again, a loud bang that shook the stairs, and she nearly screamed.

Cassidy ran to the room, ran because if she didn't race upstairs right then and see what it was, she would run out of the house and never come back.

Her bedroom door was standing open. She was breathing so hard, at first she didn't notice the breeze coming through the window. The curtains were moving; that's what made her see it and realize.

I shut that window. She was sure. Last night, when the house seemed so empty and she'd felt completely unprotected and vulnerable, she had shut the bedroom window and locked it. And now the wind was blowing through. The wind made the door slam. Like the slamming of her heart.

Someone had been here, in this room.

YOU WON'T BE SCARED . . . *NOT*
AND YOU'LL *SCREAM* FOR MORE!
Bone-chilling horror from Z-FAVE

SCREAM #1: BLOOD PACT (4355, $3.50)

Jamie Fox and her friends decide to fake a "suicide" pact when they find out their hang out, an old train depot, is going to be demolished. They sign their names in blood, but of course, never really intend to kill themselves.

Now, one by one, the signers of the pact begin to die in what looks like suicide. But Jamie suspects murder, and will be the next to die . . . unless she can unmask the cunning killer who's watching her every move!

SCREAM #2: DEADLY DELIVERY (4356, $3.50)

Derek Cliver and his friends have recently joined The Terror Club, an exciting new mail-order club, which allows them the fantasy of "disposing" of those that they despise with monsters of their own creation. But now the game is terrifyingly real because these monsters have come to life—and are actually killing.

The body count is rising as Derek and his friends somehow must undo what they've done . . . before they become the next victims!

SCREAM #3: WANTED TO RENT (4357, $3.50)

Sixteen-year-old Christy Baker is really worried. There is something about her family's handsome boarder that gives her the creeps. Things get even creepier when she finds a length of rope, masking tape, newspaper clippings about murdered women . . . and a photo of herself . . . in his room.

Now Christy is home alone. The downstairs door has just opened. She knows who's come in—and why he's there!

Available wherever paperbacks are sold, or order direct from the Publisher. Send cover price plus 50¢ per copy for mailing and handling to Penguin USA, P.O. Box 999, c/o Dept. 17109, Bergenfield, NJ 07621. Residents of New York and Tennessee must include sales tax. DO NOT SEND CASH.

SOMEONE'S WATCHING

Jessica Pierce

Z·FAVE
KENSINGTON PUBLISHING CORP.

*To Chris, my adventurer and super sleuth,
with love and thanks for all your help.*

ZEBRA BOOKS are published by

Kensington Publishing Corp.
475 Park Avenue South
New York, NY 10016

Copyright © 1994 by Jessica Pierce

All rights reserved. No part of this book may be reproduced in any form or by any means without the prior written consent of the Publisher, excepting brief quotes used in reviews.

If you purchased this book without a cover you should be aware that this book is stolen property. It was reported as "unsold and destroyed" to the Publisher and neither the Author nor the Publisher has received any payment for this "stripped book."

Z-FAVE and the Z-FAVE logo are trademarks of Kensington Publishing Corp.

First Printing: May, 1994

Printed in the United States of America

Prologue

She saw it happen, saw the man with the knife. Heard her mother's screams. She watched from the swing, waiting to be pushed. The park was empty, except for the two people struggling in the moonlight. She saw him lift his arm, holding the silvery knife in his hand. And when his arm came down. . . . She saw it all.

When the man was gone and her mother's voice was silenced, the two-year-old slipped off the swing and came alone into the wide and terrifying place. She didn't cry, because she couldn't. Like her mother, she was silent.

Huddling against the body, she tried to curl into arms that couldn't hold her. But she needed to be close. She crawled on top of her mother and sat there all night.

No one comforted her. No one stilled her trembling. She was cold and alone. Darkness was an animal that swallowed her. Her tiny fingers gripped her mother's clothes. She waited, eyes wide and staring into the face of night. Inside the beast of fear.

One

"Slow down. Please, slow down!"

The pickup took the curves too fast. It was after midnight, closed-coffin dark, and no streetlights anywhere on the winding foothill roads. Even with the best of drivers, it would have been a scary ride. But Cassidy didn't have the best. She had asked the wrong person to bring her home from the party. Brian had been drinking, and now his truck was swerving all over the road.

"I'm okay. Gimme a break," said Brian. "You sound like my mother."

"I mean it, Bri. Slow down, or stop the car. Let me out. You shouldn't be driving. You don't know what you're—"

Brian twisted around to argue with her, turning the steering wheel. The pickup veered sharply to the right. Cassidy had an instant close-up of the six-foot cyclone fence. She heard the loud snap as the headlight broke, felt the impact of grinding metal into the chain link of the fence, folding it onto the bumper.

Brian yelled. Cassidy registered that sound, but her eyes stared at the impending brick wall. In the instant before they hit, she saw herself dead. The truck would smash into it straight on at fifty miles an hour, and she would die. It wasn't panic she felt, but certainty.

Brian spun the steering wheel to the left. The truck swerved back toward the road, shearing off a corner of the brick retaining wall. Cassidy heard the crack, and thought it might have been her skull smashing on that unyielding wall. Her pulse pumped loudly in her ears, muffling the other sounds: Brian's yelling, the high squealing scream of brakes, the noise of her world coming to an end. . . .

The pickup tore out the wooden two-by-four of a rural mailbox and slammed finally into the steel post of the stop sign at the street corner. The truck didn't have any working seat belts. Brian's head hit the windshield first, shattering the glass into knife-size shards. Most of the windshield popped out when his body crashed through. Cassidy's pink ski jacket was on her lap. It was in her hands, shielding her face, as she was flung out of the passenger seat, hit the crumpled hood of Brian's pickup, and landed on the unyielding macadam.

Pain. There was nothing else.

"Cassidy . . . Cassidy!" Brian's scream cut through the blanket of hurt.

She couldn't see anything. The dark had folded around them. Brian was hidden. It was hard to move. Her body hurt—head, back, arms, and legs. A porch light flared in the hills above them. A woman shouted, "There's an accident, George. Call 911."

"Cassidy," Brian cried again. "Don't be dead. Oh, God. Where are you? I can't see you."

"I'm here."

She tried to move, but fear overwhelmed her. *They'd come so close.* Her legs shook so badly she couldn't stand. She struggled to her knees and crawled across the road, following the sound of Brian's voice. It was loud and panicky.

"Cassidy, I'm all blood. I think I'm dying."

"I'm coming to you, Bri," she told him. "Don't move."

More porch lights silhouetted a dim shape at the side of the road. Every movement hurt her back, neck, and head, but she kept crawling toward him. When close, she could see the dark smear covering his face, and knew it was blood.

"Cassidy, I'm sorry." His hand was cold and shaking. "Are you hurt? What did I do? Are you hurt?"

"I'm okay."

She put her padded jacket under Brian's head. In the distance, she could hear the wail of sirens. More lights burned into the dark, and she saw the dim outline of people running toward them from the few nearby houses. A man yelled, "There's gonna be dead ones here. Look at that truck."

The sounds and scene blurred into the hum of a black haze, like the fading of a nightmare. For a moment Cassidy saw something else in that shadowy light, something that scared her worse than the wreck. It was a vision of another night . . . when she had watched the light fade, and the folding arms of dark bring a secret terror. And death.

"Cassidy, look at me." A man was standing over her. "I'm Officer John Terrell. We're going to transport you to the hospital. Cassidy?"

"Brian's hurt," she said. "His head—"

"We've taken your friend to the ambulance."

She was confused. How could that have happened while she was right here? How could she not have known? And how did this policeman know her name?

She stared at the man's face, held into remaining consciousness only by the intense stare of his eyes. She tried to stay alert, tried to hear him, but it was too hard. The questions faded, until the only sound Cassidy heard was the hum of a heavy pulse in her ears, growing louder and louder. The last thing she saw was the policeman's face directly above her, and his eyes blending into solid black.

The emergency room was bright lights, obtrusive noise, people in orange and green uniforms, and Cassidy strapped head, shoulders, and waist to a backboard. The high frame of a neck brace wrapped around her throat. Now, she felt some of Brian's panic.

"I don't want to be here," she tried to tell them. "I'm all right." Her mom and dad would be so mad when they knew she'd been in the truck with someone who'd been drinking, and that she'd been in this accident. She didn't want her mom to see her strapped to a board like a corpse. "Get me out of this!" she yelled. "I'm going home."

"You're staying in the hospital." The cop was still there. "What made you get in a car with a drunk driver? Do you know how close you came to being killed? Don't you have any better sense than that?"

"Don't yell at me. Leave me alone," Cassidy yelled back at him. Her head hurt. She was scared and alone with this man who was shouting at her. She didn't know where Brian was, maybe he was badly hurt. Her mom and dad were going to have a fit when they heard about this.

"Cassidy," the cop's voice sounded kinder now. "Are you feeling worse? Is your back—"

"Go away. Leave me alone," she said miserably. She wished the whole thing could disappear, like the vision she'd had . . . but she knew it wouldn't.

"Oh, my God!" Mom's voice. Cassidy couldn't turn to look because her head was held immobile on the backboard. She couldn't see, but she knew. "Cassi," her mom said, "look at you. There's blood all over you."

"It's Brian's blood. I'm okay. Don't cry, Mom. Please, don't cry."

Her mom always worried too much about everything. She was older than most of Cassidy's friends' mothers by about twenty years, about a hundred times more nervous, and had a thing about trying to protect her daughter. Right now, Mom sounded scared to death.

In spite of all her anger at Brian for doing this to her, at the mean cop who wouldn't stop yelling at her, and at the hospital that wouldn't let her go home, it wasn't until she saw the fear on her mother's face that Cassidy broke down. She started crying, and couldn't stop.

Her dad was there. The two of them stood like statues staring down at her, their faces looking scared and vulnerable. Old. They didn't deserve this.

"I'm sorry," she said again and again, until the words seemed to flow together without stopping. Her mother leaned over her like a bird spreading its wing above an injured chick. She brushed a kiss across the swelling on Cassidy's forehead. Feeling the nearness of her father, and the comfort of her mother's touch, Cassidy at last felt safe.

She closed her eyes. In the stillness of that moment, she heard her father say to someone, "John, what are you doing here? I thought we made it clear that you're never to come near her."

"I took the call, Burke. It was nothing more than that."

"Stay away from Cassidy," her father said. "You're not wanted around our daughter."

"You've made your feelings known. You don't need to be worried, Burke. I didn't know it was Cassidy until I got to the scene. Once I was there, I had to help."

"She doesn't need your help. Ever."

Cassidy wished she could see their faces. She had never heard her father speak that way to anyone.

And he was talking to the policeman who'd been at the accident. She knew, because her father had called him John.

I'm Officer John Terrell.

Why was her father so mad? And even stranger, how had this cop known Cassidy by name?

"Who's Dad talking to?"

When her mother looked, Cassidy saw recognition, and then anger in her mother's eyes. "No one," said Mary Thornton. "No one at all."

In the weeks that followed the accident, Brian recovered from his injuries. The crash had totaled his pickup, and nearly totaled Brian's and Cassidy's lives as well. His license was suspended until he turned eighteen in another year, and he was fined five thousand dollars, sentenced to traffic school, and given probation instead of jail time, because it was a first offense.

Brian had cracked his elbow when hitting the windshield, and a concussion kept him in the hospital for the next three days. His face had been lacerated by glass shards, but he would live, and so would Cassidy.

"I'm never doing anything that stupid again," he swore to her when she visited him in the hospital.

"Don't worry. I don't think they'll be letting you near anything that drives," she told him.

"Okay by me. I'd be scared to get behind the wheel of a car right now, anyway. Cassidy, I feel awful about what happened, I mean to you. When I think what could have—"

"Hey, I don't want to go over it again. Okay? It's done. It was a stupid move, Bri. But look, we're both older and smarter now. I'm glad you're going to be all right."

"I'm grateful we're alive," he said, and she could see by the expression on his face that he was still shook-up over being the one responsible for the accident. This was a wound that would take longer to heal than any broken bones or concussion.

When she left the hospital, she knew they both had scars that others couldn't see. Brian's guilt was over what his drinking had caused. Cassidy had the memory of the crash. It haunted her.

Linked with the vivid memory of the accident was another, an image that had flashed in her mind just before the police and ambulance sirens forced the vision back into the dark. She had seen the approach of death for someone, watched it closing in like the lowering of an arm, and knew with absolute certainty that she'd seen it all, and been right there . . . if she could only remember.

Two

Cassidy Thornton screamed.

The light switched on. "Cassidy, wake up. It's all right, honey. You're safe. We're here with you."

Through eyes squinted against the sudden brightness, Cassidy saw her mother's face. Mary Thornton was dressed in a white cotton nightgown and pink flannel robe. Her feet were bare, and her hair was a puzzle of unfamiliar angles rearranged by sleep.

"Mom, I—"

"It was another bad dream?"

"So awful." Cassidy's face was damp. Her nightgown clung to her skin from the sweat of fear. "Why does it keep happening? Why do I keep having the same nightmare? Over and over, ever since the accident, I dream about someone being killed. When is it going to stop? What's wrong with me? Mom, I'm scared."

The tall shape of her father filled the doorway. "Mary, this has gone on too long. It's time we told her the truth. She has to know."

"Know what?" Cassidy looked from her father to her mother, and saw the worried expressions on their faces. "What are you talking about? What truth?"

"Burke, don't." Her mother's voice was sharp with alarm.

Her father crossed the room to Cassidy's bed. "I'm not going to stand by and let our daughter be destroyed by this. God knows I don't want to hurt you, Mary, but this secret has to be told. Look what it's doing to her. How many times in the last three months has she woken up screaming? Is that what you want? Is any secret so important that it's worth this?"

The nightmares had been terrible, images of dark and unseen danger, but this moment was real. Her mother was upset, and her father's face was . . . her father looked afraid. That scared Cassidy more than anything else, seeing fear in her father's eyes.

Inside, a feeling of pressure began, rising as if from the soles of Cassidy's feet to the crown of her head, pushing at her skin. Her thoughts raced, struggling to surface. She didn't ask questions, but watched his eyes. When her father sat at the corner of the bed and began to tell her, she wanted him to stop. But there were no words, because she needed to know it all.

She tried hard to understand what he was saying. The thoughts wouldn't fit. It was like a jigsaw puzzle with the wrong pieces. What he was telling her couldn't be true.

"I'm not your daughter?"

"Of course you're our daughter," cried her

mother, hugging Cassidy to her so fiercely that the loving arms hurt. "Are you happy with your truth now, Burke?"

Cassidy felt as if she were smothering, and pushed free of her mother's grip. "I'm not your child? Is that what you mean? Did Mom give birth to me, or didn't she?"

For once, her mother didn't speak. That was an answer.

"You're our daughter, Cassidy," her father said, "you always will be, but you're our adopted child."

It was too much to take in at once. "I can't believe this. Why would you keep it from me?" she asked, feeling stunned. "When did you adopt me? Right after I was born?"

"No," her father said. "You were two."

"Two!" That seemed worse. She hadn't been a baby, but a little kid. "I was that old, and my mother didn't want me?"

"Cassidy," he said, "that's not how it was."

"Then how was it? What was wrong with me? Was I so terrible?" She was feeling hurt and betrayed. Everything she'd understood about her life had changed. Her parents weren't her parents. She wasn't who she'd always thought she was. In fact, she didn't know anything about herself. "Didn't my real mother love me? Why would she give me away after keeping me for two years?"

"She didn't give you away," her father explained. "Your mother died."

"Died?" She had just been given knowledge

about a parent she hadn't known, and now that parent was taken from her. "How?"

"She was murdered."

The air seemed too thin to breathe. A single question had to be asked. "Who killed my mother?"

Her father looked away. "We don't know. The case was never solved. You were the only witness."

It was as if a door had slammed and Cassidy was locked inside herself with these words. Her terror had come true. The haunting images of her dreams had forced their way into her waking life. No morning sunlight would make the nightmares vanish. Now, there was no escape.

"That is so weird," said Rory.

Rory Spencer had been Cassidy's best friend since fifth grade. They had gone through the traumas of puberty, junior high, and first dates together. There wasn't anything about Cassidy that Rory didn't know—at least, nothing Cassidy didn't know about herself. This was different.

Rory leaned back against the headboard of Cassidy's bed, her rust-colored hair falling loosely over her shoulders. "Did they tell you her name?"

"Whose name?"

"Your real mother's."

It sounded so strange. "No, my . . . Mom got upset, and Dad stopped talking about it."

"Great," said Rory. "Drop a bombshell like this one and then clam up. How mature."

"You know my dad," said Cassidy. "He gives in

to my mother on everything. Maybe later, when she calms down a little."

"Are you kidding? You want to wait that long?"

"No, but what else can I do?"

Rory picked up the phone. "I know someone who can help us."

"Someone?"

"Matt Austin. His father's a private detective. Matt's learned all this stuff about investigations because of his dad. He's planning to be a PI after he graduates. He's pretty good at it already."

Cassidy felt a quickening in her pulse. "I can't pay him. Do you think he'd be interested in helping us for free?"

"We won't know unless we ask. What do you have to lose?"

Cassidy wished Rory hadn't put it that way. There might be a lot to lose, maybe her whole family. "Okay," she agreed, "call Matt."

"Finding missing people is easy," said Matt. "Finding a killer could be a little harder."

Matt Austin, a senior at La Cañada High, was tall, thin, and good-looking, if you liked the lanky, athletic build of swimmers and tennis players. His ready grin spoke for a healthy self-confidence, promising he could accomplish anything. Looking into Matt's green eyes—like deep grasslands with gold flecks of tiger light in them, and dark cages of lashes around all that wildness—Cassidy was ready to believe.

"Look, I don't expect you to find the killer," said Cassidy. "Even the police couldn't do that. What I want is to find out more about my real mother, and more about what happened."

"No problem," Matt said. "I can help you."

"Really?" She was beginning to feel a rush of anticipation. She glanced at Rory.

"Sure," said Matt. "All I need to get started is a few pieces of information, like your mother's name, birth date, and social security number."

The eagerness faded. "I don't know her social security number, or her birth date. I don't even know her name."

Cassidy felt frustrated and embarrassed. "C'mon, Rory. This was a dumb idea. Let's go."

"Wait a minute." Matt touched Cassidy's arm. "I didn't say I had to have all that. I only meant it would make things easier."

She turned to face him. "You can still find out about her?"

"Absolutely."

She wasn't so sure. "You're not making this up, are you?"

"No way."

"Hey, if Matt is willing to help us," Rory backed him up, "why not give him a chance?"

Cassidy couldn't explain how she was feeling, the tightness in her chest, the skittering over her nerves, like steel wool over teeth fillings. Maybe Rory couldn't understand. Maybe no one could. Still, they had come to Matt for help.

"Okay," Cassidy agreed. "Where do we start?"

There was that grin on Matt's face again. "We start at the beginning."

"I told you, I don't know anything about—"

"Take it easy. I mean your beginning. When were you born?"

"Me?"

"You're the one we're talking about."

"August ninth."

"And you're sixteen?"

She nodded.

He calculated back for the year. "Okay, with your birth date, we can go into the Hall of Records and trace your mother's name."

"Just like that?" It was hard to believe it could be so simple.

"It should be there. All births are supposed to be recorded. Where were you born?"

"I'm not sure. My mom always said I was born at Huntington Hospital in Pasadena, but what if she told me the wrong place? What if she didn't know where I was born? I was two when I was adopted."

The word *adopted* sounded so foreign, as if she were describing someone else. All certainness had disappeared from Cassidy's life. She didn't know anything about herself anymore.

"We'll check it out," said Matt. "The Hall of Records is the best place to start. Meanwhile, try to get your parents to give you a few more details. Ask them the name of the agency they used, and what date your adoption became official."

Cassidy nodded, but she wasn't sure her parents

would tell her anything else. Her mom had been so upset since the night her dad had told about the adoption, she'd been avoiding Cassidy lately, as if Cassidy had done something wrong.

"I know you're shook-up about all this," said Matt, "but people find out they're adopted all the time. It's a shock at first, but it's not such a big deal. Quit worrying. We'll find out about you."

That's what scared Cassidy. She knew Matt was trying to reassure her, but she was the daughter of a woman who'd been killed, and the only witness to the murder. What if Matt helped her find the answers? Would the answers lead to her mother's killer? And worse, was the killer waiting for her to remember?

"Stewart, I'm concerned about her."

Cassidy was passing through the hall outside the kitchen when she overheard her father's phone conversation. His words caught her attention. She knew he was talking about her. She stopped and listened.

"I guess the accident triggered memories," her father said. "The nightmares she's been having remind me of the ones she had as a child. That time was so traumatic for her. Remember, she wouldn't speak and didn't seem to notice anything or anyone? You helped her through it and she got better. For years, she's done well, without any problem. We thought it was behind us," he said, "but now the dreams are back. Since the accident, she's woken up screaming nearly every night. The nightmares are getting worse, and more frequent. Mary and I don't know what to do, Stewart. You've got to help us."

Cassidy stepped into the kitchen, anger pumping heat into her veins. "Dad!"

He turned and saw her. "Tuesday at four is fine," he said quickly. "Thank you, Stewart. Goodbye."

"It's private," Cassidy cried. "You're talking to someone about me, and it's private!"

"I know, honey. But Stewart's not just anyone. Dr. Randall has seen you before, Cassidy."

"He's a doctor?"

Her father nodded.

"When did he see me?"

"A long time ago . . . when you were four. He knows your case, and he's a family friend."

"A family friend? I've never heard of him."

"He's busy with his practice. We haven't seen him in years, but I trust him, Cassidy. I've made an appointment for you."

"I'm not sick. I don't need a doctor. All I need are some answers to my questions."

"I can't give you those answers, but I'm going to insist that you see Dr. Randall. He's a psychiatrist. He can help you through this."

She was stunned that her father thought she should see a psychiatrist, that he believed she needed a doctor's help. Her second reaction formed itself into a question. "I've had these dreams before?"

Her father scraped a chair back from the kitchen table and sat. He slumped forward, as if carrying a heavy weight. "When you were four, we planned to enter you into nursery school. Everything was fine until the first day. We got to the school and I tried to take you to the playground, but you started screaming."

"Screaming? Not crying? Not just scared to be going to school?"

"You were screaming, Cassidy. We had to take you home. When the screaming stopped, you were limp as a rag doll, and totally silent. You didn't speak again for days. Your mother and I were frightened we'd lose you. We took you to doctors, specialists, but all they could tell us was that you'd had a shock. They said you might never come out of it. It was Stewart who managed to reach into your silence and bring you back to us. Now do you understand why I'm so anxious for you to see him? I can't take the chance of losing you again."

Cassidy tried to imagine herself the way her father described her, four years old and so terrified of something, she'd become mute. Part of her didn't want to think about it, didn't want to remember anything. But part of her was drawn to it with a wary fascination. He was talking about events from her childhood, something that had scarred her mind so deeply, she'd reacted this way.

She kept imagining that little girl, herself, paralyzed with fear. Questions formed in her mind. She needed answers. "Did Dr. Randall explain why I acted like that? What was wrong with me?"

"He said you'd slipped back into the silent world you'd hidden in before we adopted you."

"What does that mean?" It was as if the familiar knit of Cassidy's life were unraveling, and she felt herself disappearing into loosening threads. This child her father described was a stranger, someone she didn't know or remember, and yet it was she.

"When you came to live with us, you didn't speak."

"Maybe I was too young. Lots of kids don't talk much until they're two, or even older. Maybe I was slow."

"No, you were very bright, believe me." He was so proud of her. She could see it in his eyes. "Before your mother's death, you were speaking in long, complicated sentences. And you could count. You knew your numbers and the letters of the alphabet. You were smarter than any of the other kids."

Cassidy was amazed, not by what she had done as a two-year-old, but that her father was the one telling her about it. "How do you know all that stuff? Did the adoption agency tell you?"

"No one had to tell us, honey. We knew you from the day you were born."

She was startled by this revelation. It took her a moment to comprehend what her father was saying.

"Then, you knew my mother."

It was as if a door had slammed between them. Cassidy knew she'd asked too much, pushed too hard. Her father reacted by shoving back his chair and walking to the doorway, putting a distance between them.

"I'm sorry. Don't be mad," she said. "I want to know about her. That's all. Can't you understand? I need to know what happened."

"You have an appointment to see Dr. Randall at four o'clock the day after tomorrow. We're not going to talk about this anymore, Cassidy. It's best. I've said too much."

"Dad, please."

He left her then, alone and falling through a dark drop of fear. Why were there so many secrets? What were they afraid she'd find out? Her father had pulled away, and her mother was avoiding her.

Cassidy was lost between them. And she knew something else. That little girl who had witnessed her mother's death was still hidden in the world of silence.

Three

The Austin home was in a more expensive neighborhood than Cassidy's. Her house was one story; Matt's was two. Her dad mowed his own lawn; the Austins had a gardener. And by the looks of their furniture, expensive wallpaper, and window treatments, they had a decorator, too. Cassidy's mom had picked the drapes and furniture for their house. Nothing was perfectly matched like it was at Matt's, but Cassidy's house felt more homey.

Matt's long legs were hooked over the side of a chair in his living room, his feet propped on the upholstered arm of the adjoining sofa. Cassidy's mom would be fuming if she saw her doing that. In Matt, the pose looked casual, comfortable, easy.

"You two want to go with me to the Hall of Records?" he asked.

Rory had come with her. She knew Matt a lot better than Cassidy did, and Rory was the one who'd suggested asking him for help in the first place.

"Would you mind?" asked Cassidy. "I'd like to be there if you find anything."

"Want to go now?" he offered. "It's four o'clock. They'll be open for another hour."

"Could we?"

"Sure."

It was Monday. Sitting in school all morning and afternoon had been agony. Whatever Cassidy had been taught in her classes today had competed with thoughts of finding out her mother's identity. Algebra and biology hadn't stood a chance. All day she'd imagined coming to Matt's house, going with him to the Hall of Records, and opening the door to her past.

"I would have gone by myself in a day or two," Matt told them. "I hadn't forgotten."

"She's anxious," said Rory.

"Since I found out I was adopted, it's all I can think about," Cassidy admitted. "I want to know about my real mother—who she was, what she was like, and all that."

"C'mon, then. What are we waiting for?" he asked. "Let's get started."

They drove in Matt's black Acura through the theater and restaurant district of Old Town, to Pasadena's Hall of Records. The city offices were housed in a formal courtyard of elaborate buildings, including Old City Hall, the Hall of Records, the Health Department, and various other municipal buildings. The dome of City Hall was impressive and intimidating.

"Are you sure they'll let us inside?" Rory asked.

"It's public access," said Matt. "They don't have a choice."

Cassidy didn't ask any questions. She followed Matt's lead and kept her nervousness to herself. Rory was right, she was anxious. And scared. Opening a door to information and knowledge meant you could never close that door again. Whatever secrets her parents had kept to protect her, once discovered, could never be put back in place and hidden. It was like the old proverb: Be careful what you ask for; you just might get it.

Matt led them through the maze of hallways and doors. From his familiarity with the layout of the offices, it was obvious he'd been here before and knew his way around. Cassidy would have followed him into the mayor's office, if he'd steered them that way, but Rory hesitated.

"Where are you taking us?" she asked, coming to an abrupt stop like a mule that wouldn't be budged.

"This corridor leads to the microfiche room of the Hall of Records," Matt explained.

"Hold on a minute," said Rory. "Are we supposed to be here? I mean, couldn't we get in trouble for snooping around in this place?"

"It's okay," Matt assured her. "I come here with my dad all the time."

"But your dad's a private investigator. He's got reasons to be here. We're kids. Don't you think—"

"I think you should quit worrying," said Matt.

He opened the door to a room designated MICROFICHE. Inside, was a wide storeroom of microfiche machines and monitors, a row of library-style tables and chairs, and four people—

two men and two women—searching through trays of microfiche cards.

"Do you kids want something?" said a man's bureaucratic voice.

"I *told* you," whispered Rory. "Now, we're in for it."

Cassidy found it hard to take her next breath, too, but Matt seemed cool and undisturbed.

"Hi." He faced the clerk and flashed that *I'm a great guy* grin on him. "We're here on a school assignment, to write a report on which facilities are made available to public access through the state's freedom of information laws."

"Look, I don't care what report you're doing," said the clerk. "This is not a place for kids."

Rory turned around to leave, but Matt grabbed her arm. He pulled out a small tape recorder and pressed *record*. "Maybe I was misinformed about our civil rights. Could you tell me on exactly what grounds you're denying us access to these records? I'd like to submit this as part of my report to the judge."

"Judge?" The public servant's face changed color—from pasty white to a florid flush of pink. "You didn't say anything about a judge."

"Didn't I?" asked Matt, innocently. "I didn't think I needed to mention our reasons. Is that required? Please speak directly into the tape, Mr. Johnson."

The clerk stepped away from them. "No. It's not required. You go ahead and look around. Do your report. But don't mess up anything," he warned.

"I thought you said this was public access, and you come here with your dad all the time," said Rory.

"It is, and I do," said Matt. "There shouldn't be any trouble, but sometimes if you're young, they take on an attitude. You've gotta give one back, that's all. C'mon, grab a place at that machine. I'll look up the fiche cards."

"I'll help you," Cassidy told him. She didn't want Matt to find out anything about her before she saw it herself. It was weird; she felt protective of her past life, as if she were guarding that little girl.

"Okay," said Matt, pulling open the microfiche file drawer for births registered in Pasadena. He finger-walked through the weeks of July, then slowly examined the film cards for the weeks of August in Cassidy's year of birth. He pulled these cards from the file, placed them on a tray, and brought them to the table where Rory waited.

"We'd better check the surrounding weeks to be sure," explained Matt. "You might have been born a week or two before or after your assumed birth date."

The remark was made innocently enough, but struck Cassidy as if her whole existence were based on lies. Matt didn't know how this made her feel. But how could he? He was sure of his parents, his life. She wasn't.

Rory positioned the first card between the glass plates. Matt and Cassidy stood behind her chair and watched the screen.

"The records listed here are abstracts, partials of the originals. They won't contain all the information. To get that, we'll have to send away to the state capital. That can take a while. Also, sometimes the birth certificates have been pulled and sealed by the adoption agency," said Matt. "It depends on their policy."

Cassidy tried to prepare herself for disappointment. Her birth certificate would be missing, as Matt said was possible, and she would never know the identity of her real parents. She hadn't thought much about her real father until now, but seeing the names on the other birth certificates—mothers and fathers—made her want to know the identity of her birth father, too.

Rory was skimming through the births registered on August eighth. She was hurrying because they were running out of time. The microfiche room would close in ten minutes.

Matt reached for her hand. "Wait a minute. Go back one. You skipped the first entry on August ninth."

Rory moved the card and the entry appeared on the monitor. She read the information. "Live birth, female, 2:15 A.M., Huntington Hospital, born to Anne Elizabeth Logan . . . Cassidy Anne Logan. It's you." She glanced back at Cassidy. "I think we found your mother."

"No way. Man," said Matt, "too easy."

Cassidy heard them, but she was lost in other words, those printed on the birth certificate. Anne

Logan . . . Cassidy Anne. "She named me after herself, my middle name."

"Yeah, looks that way," said Matt.

"She was eighteen when you were born," said Rory. "Imagine, a year or two from our age, having a kid. Scary."

Cassidy felt a rush of closeness for her real mother in that moment. Anne Logan had been a teenager when she'd had her baby. What must it have been like, being so young, unmarried and pregnant?

"It's kind of unusual that she kept you," said Matt. "Back then, most unmarried mothers her age would have given up their babies for adoption. But she didn't. She must have had help. Relatives. Somebody."

Cassidy was overwhelmed with thoughts about her mother, thinking how hard it must have been for an eighteen-year-old, single and probably not earning much money, to try to bring up a child by herself. And that she must have loved her baby, to have named the child Anne, after herself.

"The record doesn't list your father," said Rory. "In the place for the father's name, it says *Not Indicated.*"

"That's weird," said Matt. "Usually, the father's name is listed even if the parents weren't married, so the mother will be eligible for child support. She must have hated the guy, or wanted him out of her life pretty badly, not to have named him for the birth records."

"Hey!" Rory elbowed Matt in the ribs. "Why

don't you think what you're saying before you blurt out something like that? These are her parents, you know, not just some people in a case."

"Sorry, I—"

"It's okay," Cassidy told them. "Don't jump all over him. Matt's right. There must have been a good reason for not listing my father's name."

"Maybe she was afraid of the guy," Matt suggested.

"Of my father? Why?"

"I don't know. Somebody killed her."

At once, the room seemed too small, and the thoughts in her mind too terrifying.

"You okay?" Rory asked.

She didn't know. Didn't speak.

"We're closing in five minutes," the clerk said. "The monitors will be turned off, and the microfiche cards need to go back into the files."

"Cassidy?" asked Rory.

"Take her outside," said Matt. "I'll take care of all this and meet you there in a minute."

Rory walked with her through the long corridors of the building. "C'mon," she said. "Don't make a big deal of this. Matt's only guessing. He doesn't know anything for sure. Cassi, say something. You're scaring me."

"I'm all right." That wasn't true, but Rory needed to hear it. "I wasn't expecting to hear that. It was kind of a shock, you know?"

Rory nodded. "Matt can be pretty lame sometimes."

"No, it's not his fault. He's helping me. Don't rag on him about it, okay?"

Rory didn't look convinced. "Somebody ought to set him straight. Mr. Insensitive. Jeez, get a clue."

"I mean it," Cassidy insisted. "Don't say anything to him. Promise me?"

"Fine, but let's not talk about this anymore. When I looked at you back there, your eyes were . . . like you didn't see me."

Cassidy tried to look normal for Rory's sake. "It's a lot to get used to all at once. I kind of freaked out for minute, but I'm all right. Really."

"Yeah, okay."

From behind them came the sounds of Matt running down the hall. He caught up with them at the door leading outside. "Was that great, or what? Not bad for the first day's work. Now we know your mother's name."

It was true. Cassidy had her answer. But the satisfaction she'd expected to feel after learning her mother's name had lasted only seconds. Instead, one question had been replaced by another. Now, she needed to know more: about her father, and why her mother had left his name off the birth certificate; about who killed her mother, and why; and about the reasons for her nightmares, the faces still hidden in the dark.

Four

Cassidy kept what she'd learned about her real mother to herself. She didn't tell her parents, and she didn't tell Dr. Randall. The information she'd learned on her own was personal, private, and not to be shared.

Dr. Stewart Randall's office reminded Cassidy of something from a glamorous movie. His office was in Pasadena's famous Trawler Building, the one called an "architectural fantasy" in *Pasadena* magazine. It was modern, steel and glass, looking more like a work of art than a building.

Inside, the furniture in Dr. Randall's waiting room was a blend of leather upholstery and rich woods. Oil paintings on the walls looked expensive, and the glass-fronted curio cabinet held small bronze sculptures and porcelain figurines. There were art books on the glass and chrome table, *A Day In The Life Of Ireland, The Art Of Mary Cassatt, Covered Bridges Of New England,* and *England From The Air.* These were nothing like the dog-eared magazines in the crowded waiting room of Cassidy's family doctor. She hadn't expected such a display of wealth.

"Can we afford this place?" she asked her father.

"It's all right. Stewart isn't charging us. He's seeing you for free."

"Really?" At first, she was delighted. Then curiosity turned to concern. "For free? Why would he do that?"

"I told you. He's a friend of the family."

Before Cassidy could ask any more questions, the nurse walked into the room. She wore a brown suede dress, an elaborate Zuni squash blossom necklace, and calf-high boots. No white uniform and nurse's shoes in this office. "Won't you come with me, Cassidy," she said. "Dr. Randall would like to see you."

Cassidy glanced at her dad to see if he would offer to go with her. She didn't know what to expect from a psychiatrist and was a little afraid to see this one by herself. Her dad simply nodded in the direction of the open doorway leading to Dr. Randall's office. She got up and followed the nurse through the peach-colored hallway to a spacious room with wide picture windows that let in the afternoon light.

It was impressive and intimidating. She felt nervous, guilty as a truant waiting in the vice principal's office. Outside these windows, the world looked invitingly free. In this room, she felt confined. Trapped.

"This city always looks better from up here. I stare at it, too. But that's the falsehood of looking down on things. Distance makes everything seem nicer than it really is."

He was about forty, dark-haired, and distinguished looking in a charcoal wool-blazer-and-gray-slacks kind of way. She noticed everything about him at once, absorbing it all in a single glance. Stewart Randall was tall and handsome in a way that said power and prestige. He had the lean but muscular build of a man with memberships in expensive athletic clubs, and a sensitivity to his face that must have put his patients immediately at ease and made them trust him. It was his eyes, liquid dark and soulful as a deer's in the gunsight of a hunter. Staring, he seemed able to see into her.

"The last time I saw you," he said, closing the door behind him, "you were a child. You've grown up, Cassidy."

"I'm sorry. I don't remember much about—"

"Of course you don't. You were only four." He extended his hand to her. "I'm Dr. Stewart Randall."

She shook hands with him, said hello, and then stood awkwardly.

"Come and sit down." He suggested the conversational grouping near the window, two comfortably upholstered chairs with a small table between them. On the table was a vase of flowers, a comforting arrangement. *Designed to be so,* thought Cassidy, determined to be resistant to all influence.

She didn't belong here. This was her father's idea, not hers. She wasn't crazy, even if her parents thought she was, just scared.

"Your father tells me you've been having recurring nightmares."

"It's not such a big deal. I've had bad dreams all my life."

"Have you? But these are different?"

"I don't know. Maybe."

"What do you think started these nightmares, Cassidy?"

"The accident, I guess."

"I'd like to hear about that, if you wouldn't mind telling me."

It was easier to talk about the accident than her dreams. She understood what happened in the crash. The nightmares were harder. She told Dr. Randall about trying to get Brian to slow down, hitting the stop sign, and the all-consuming dark after she'd gone through the pickup's windshield and landed on the road.

"It sounds terrifying. You might have been killed."

She nodded.

"Were you afraid of dying? Did you think about it?"

"I don't know. I thought about Brian—I was afraid he might die—and my parents. I don't think I saw myself like that."

"Like what?"

She felt pursued by his question. Hunted. "Dead."

"But you saw something that night, didn't you? Something that frightened you very much."

"Yes." She wondered how he knew this. Was he psychic? Is that why they called them psychiatrists?

"Will you tell me about it?"

"It wasn't anything important." She wanted to go home, wanted to leave this office before he made her say something she didn't want to talk about.

"I think it may be what's triggering these nightmares," said Dr. Randall. "I won't force you, if it's too hard." His voice was gentle, and he looked away for a couple of minutes, gazing out the window, giving her a chance to take a deep breath without feeling tracked by his eyes. "Do you want to stop having these nightmares, Cassidy?"

The question surprised her. "Of course. That's why I'm here."

"Is it? I think you're here because your father insisted. He did, didn't he?"

"Yes." He was reading her again, and she didn't like it. She wondered if all her emotions showed on her face.

"He's worried about you."

"I know."

"Cassidy, what are you hiding? There's something you're keeping secret, isn't there?"

"Ask my dad about secrets. Ask my mother. Ask them why they didn't tell me I was adopted."

"Oh, I might be able to help you with that. I told them not to tell you."

"What?"

"I told them to protect you from all thought of your mother's death. That included your adoption."

"Why would you do that? Lots of kids know they're adopted, and they're fine. Why couldn't I know the truth? What right did you have to tell my parents to keep secrets from me?"

"Because of the trauma caused by your mother's murder. I was thinking of you."

"Me! That's a laugh."

"Calm down and listen." His physical attitude became more intimate. He leaned closer, hands braced on his knees, his eyes staring intently into hers. "When I saw you after your mother's death, you were a severely depressed four-year-old. Nearly catatonic. Do you know what that means?"

"My dad said I didn't speak." She didn't want to talk, or have anything more to do with Dr. Randall. Anger needled her skin, giving it goose bumps.

"Your condition was much worse than not speaking," said Dr. Randall. "Have you ever seen anyone in a trance?"

"Only on TV."

"That's not the same. A real trance is a scary thing, especially in a child. It's a disconnection. Imagine that each of us has an invisible line connecting us to everyone else, so we can see, talk, and feel. But this child's line had been cut. She—you—didn't attach to anything."

"You're saying I was a vegetable?"

"No, I'm sure you had thoughts, but you didn't share them. You retreated to a world of separateness and silence. That's one of the reasons I want you to share your thoughts with me now, to keep that line open. You have a tendency to shut down when things frighten you, Cassidy."

What he was saying bothered her. It was true, she had been scared by what she'd remembered on the night of the crash, the image of a man in the dark, his arm rising and falling . . . and because she'd been scared, she hadn't talked about it.

"Do the nightmares mean I'm going back into cata—"

"No, probably not."

She would have preferred *absolutely not*. "But, it might happen again?"

"Not likely."

Now, she was scared. "What if the nightmares get worse? What if I start acting weird, but no one notices? Could I—"

"Cassidy, I don't want you to worry about this. I'm here to help you."

She'd felt a lot better before she came into this office. "I want to know about my mother."

Dr. Randall glanced at his watch. "I'm sorry. We'll have to continue our talk next week. My five o'clock patient will be waiting to see me. I want you to think about what scared you so much on the night of the car accident, and what you remember of your dreams. You can't close those memories away, Cassidy. It isn't healthy, and it won't work. Whatever's frightening you will surface in your dreams. Sooner or later, you'll know what it is. I want to be there to help you when that time comes."

"But can't you tell me what happened on the night my mother died?"

"I don't think that would be a good idea. Maybe later. Right now, I'm not sure you could handle it."

"I can handle a lot more than you think. I know my mother's name was Anne Logan." She instantly wished she hadn't said it.

"Who told you that?"

"No one."

"Cassidy, don't lie to me."

"I don't lie. And I don't like people who accuse me of it."

He seemed to think that over. "All right, we'll leave that question for now. What else do you know?"

"Not much, but I'm going to find out. You and my parents can't keep this a big secret from me. I'm going to keep searching for information. I want to know the truth. You can't stop me."

Dr. Randall leaned back in his chair. His brows formed a scowling V-shape. "That would be a very foolish thing to do. Whoever murdered your mother is still free. Do you realize what that means? The killer knows you were there. Don't pry into something that might hurt you, Cassidy. It isn't safe."

All her courage vanished. In its place were the doctor's words. *The killer knows you were there.*

That night, Matt met them at Rory's house.

"What's next?" Rory asked. "We've got the name. Where do we go from here?"

"We need to apply for a copy of the complete birth certificate," said Matt. "It's kept on record at the state capital. There's a fee required."

"What will that tell us?" Cassidy wanted answers, but she didn't know what Matt had in mind.

"Just about everything we need to know. There should be a lot more information on the original document than there was on the abstract in the microfiche files. Most important, it may list your mother's social security number. That's the real ticket to information."

"Why?" asked Cassidy.

"With her number, we can ask the right questions of the social security office. You can follow a person's life through those little numbers. Addresses and phone numbers change, people drop husbands and wives, they leave their jobs, but they never abandon their social security number—unless we're talking about someone criminally intent on changing his or her identity, or someone the feds are protecting."

"Come on," Rory reacted skeptically. "You're talking about government offices. Those clerks will make Mr. Johnson look friendly. They won't tell us anything. A person's social security information is like some sacred trust. The government protects all that stuff—don't they?"

Matt didn't look so sure. "Do they?"

Everything was moving too fast. Cassidy suddenly wanted her world to slow down. She needed to absorb the shock of what she'd heard earlier today. Maybe Dr. Randall was right. Maybe she couldn't handle it.

All this was leading to the day of her mother's death. The closer she came to finding out about that day, the more scared she became. Right now, she wished she could freeze this moment until she felt stronger, more ready to deal with it.

Rory had no such reluctance. She prodded Matt's contagious self-confidence. "You mean we could call the local social security office and ask for the information we need, and they'll give it to us?"

"Only if we ask the right questions."

She shook her head. "C'mon, Matt. Yesterday was a lucky break. You didn't really believe Cassidy's birth certificate would be in those microfiche files, did you?"

"No," he admitted. "I figured it would be sealed by the courts, because of the adoption."

"Okay, so let's be honest. I don't want you getting Cassidy's hopes up for nothing. Look at her."

He looked. Cassidy glanced away, embarrassed by this closer scrutiny of her feelings.

"This is serious to her," Rory warned him. "You're talking a whole other game with the social security numbers. As if one of us knows what to ask."

"That would be me," said Matt. "It's called a ruse. My dad uses them all the time."

"What's a ruse?" asked Rory.

"You know, conversation that makes them think

you're somebody who's got a right to know whatever it is you're asking."

Cassidy needed to understand. "These ruses, are they legal?"

"On the edge, but don't worry, we won't cross the line."

"Great," said Rory. "That makes me feel *so* much better."

Cassidy turned on her. "Rory, cut it out."

Matt stood, ready to leave. "Look," he told Rory angrily, "you asked for my help. If you want me to stop, just say so."

Cassidy didn't give Rory a chance to answer. "No, I want to go ahead with this. Please, keep helping me."

"Okay," Matt agreed. "For you."

After that, Matt was quiet, and Rory sulked for the rest of the night, but at least they didn't argue. The silence was a welcome change. It gave Cassidy a chance to think.

Her mother was like the dream, an image covered in layers that Cassidy couldn't see through or understand. With Matt's help, she was going to remove those layers, one by one. Then what would she see? Her mother's face? Her father? Or the eyes of a murderer?

Five

Matt filed with the state for a copy of Cassidy's birth certificate, but said it would take a couple of weeks before the copy arrived in the mail. He put his address on the return envelope, so it wouldn't be delivered to Cassidy's house.

"What do we do now?" asked Rory. "Wait?"

"No way," said Matt.

They were in the school quad, their usual place during lunch break, hanging out by the benches under the shade of the blooming jacaranda tree. Its petals were spilled across the benches and ground like lavender snow.

Cassidy admired Matt's assertiveness, but he wasn't dealing with the dreams she'd been having. No one knew about them. She'd kept them to herself, secretly wondering if she were getting worse and slipping closer to that trancelike state Dr. Randall had warned her about. The dreams were so real, and they wouldn't stop.

She'd be seeing Dr. Randall again on Thursday. A regular appointment, her dad called it. There was nothing regular or ordinary about the way it made her feel, dreading the next visit ever since last week. Maybe that's why the dreams were so much worse. If Matt and Rory weren't helping her, she might have given up the struggle for information. It was beginning to scare her.

"I thought we had to wait for the social security number?" said Rory.

"I don't plan to sit around and wait," said Matt. "There are lots of things we can find out before that."

"Like what?" Rory asked.

"Like . . . how do you think your mother voted, Cassidy? Democrat or Republican?"

"Huh?" was Rory's reaction.

"Are you serious?" asked Cassidy. "How would I know?"

"Exactly. We're going to find out."

"We are? How? And why?"

"The county courthouse keeps a file of voter registration records. If your mother voted in any election, it'll be there."

She was impressed by his resource information, but unsure of what difference it would make. "So I find out she voted for Jimmy Carter—how does that help us?"

"Voter registration cards list the person's current address. We can find out where she lived."

It was like pieces of a puzzle, the scattered bits of her mother's life. Matt and Rory were helping her find them. Once the bits were put together, Cassidy was going to know a lot about her mother, and maybe about herself, too.

"You're amazing," she said to Matt. "You ought to charge a fee."

"Don't worry. I'm planning to ask something for my services."

The comment earned a long stare between her and Rory.

"I've got some time after school. You want to go today?"

"Sure," Cassidy said. "How about you, Rory?"

"Can't. I'm working at the video store this afternoon."

Cassidy and Matt agreed to meet in the school parking lot after classes. All through algebra she wondered about where her mother had lived. If it was nearby, she could go there. Maybe it was a place she'd lived with her mother, a house she'd recognize, a neighborhood.

It wasn't easy to put such thoughts out of her mind and concentrate on schoolwork. In the last couple of weeks, her grades had really slipped. She'd earned a C minus on her last biology quiz, and didn't have a clue to what the teacher was talking about in algebra. The dreams had been the cause at first. Since she'd found out she was adopted and about her mother's death, nothing else seemed to matter. She was caught up in it, like being obsessed. She had to understand what happened.

The county courthouse was in downtown Los Angeles, a long drive from Pasadena. It was an old building, in an area of L.A. that felt unfamiliar and unsafe. She was glad Matt was with her. He seemed to know his way around.

The county registrar's office was on the sixth floor. They walked in, and a man not much older than Matt asked, "Could I help you?"

Matt had his ruse down pat. "We're taking a voters' survey of a percentage of the residents in our area."

"Uh-huh," said the man. His eyes did a kind of fade-out, his initial interest in them turning to boredom at the mention of a survey.

"What we need today is a copy of the voter registration for one of the residents on our survey. You know how it is," he said. "Everything has to be an official document for the officials at the top of the ladder to accept it."

The clerk nodded his agreement. "Oh, I know. They don't care how much work it makes for anyone else, as long as they get their documents in hand."

Matt smiled. "We're just starting out. I'm sure you could tell us a lot about it."

"I sure could," said the clerk. "I'll be back in a minute—what's the name?"

"Anne Logan." It made Cassidy feel strange to say her mother's name. Somehow, it was as if every time she said it, she was drawing her mother closer.

"Worked like a charm," said Matt, after the clerk left.

"Smooth," she agreed.

He came back a few minutes later, with two Xeroxed slips of paper in his hand. "If you need an authorized copy of the originals, you'll have to send a check to the courthouse."

"No, these are fine." He took the copies from the clerk. "You have a good day," Matt told him, as they walked out of the office.

The indifferent expression on the clerk's face said he probably wouldn't.

Cassidy's hand was shaking when she held the first page before her and tried to read the small print. Her mother had registered as a Democrat for the election. That pleased Cassidy. Her political leanings were the same.

She saw Anne Logan's signature at the bottom of the page, neat and legible, with no flourish to any of the letters. It was the way Cassidy wrote her name, too. Plain. Sensible. These were small connections, but linked them.

"What's the address?" asked Matt.

She'd forgotten to look at that. "Four-eighteen Raymond Street."

"That's in Old Town," said Matt.

"I don't remember any apartments or houses in that neighborhood. It's all restaurants, shops, and businesses."

"Maybe it is now, but look at the date. This was sixteen years ago. Things change in a city in that amount of time. There might still be someone around who remembers something about your mother, or the place she lived. We'll drive by and check."

Sixteen years ago, her mother had just turned

eighteen. It must have been the first election in which she could vote. Cassidy was disappointed. She'd hoped the address would lead them to a home she'd remember. It was frustrating to think that even the place where her mother had lived was gone.

"What's it say on the second page?"

She glanced at the form. It was dated two years later, for a county election. The address was different. "Two-twenty-four Oak Knoll." It sounded familiar, but she didn't know why. "Could we go to this one right now?"

"Sure. I'll check my *Thomas Guide* for directions."

They drove in a silence that was punctuated with racing thoughts. Cassidy's mind was flooded with feelings she didn't understand. It was as if she were split down the middle. One side of her was yearning to learn everything she could about a mother she couldn't remember, and the other side was afraid of what she'd find out.

Even driving to see the house scared her. She used to live there with her mother. It was part of her life, but something awful had happened to end all that. Would she see the house and remember everything?

"Are you okay?" Matt stopped for a red light. There was concern for her in his eyes, and in the gentle tone of his voice.

"You think I'm doing the right thing?" she asked. "I mean, digging up the past . . . maybe I should leave it alone."

"Is that what you want? We don't have to drive

by the house. I don't want to push you into anything, Cassidy. If it's getting to you, we can stop right now."

"But I want to know. It's just . . . I guess I'm scared."

"Of what?"

"Dr. Randall said, 'Don't pry into something that might hurt you.' He told me whoever killed my mother is still free. Maybe someone's watching me, knows what I'm doing. Everything that brings me closer to my mother makes me feel like I'm getting closer to the killer, too."

Matt drove the car through the intersection and parked along a nearby curb. "You've been seeing Dr. Randall to help get you through this, right?"

She nodded, not wanting to tell him about the nightmares.

"It seems to me—and I'm not a doctor—but it seems to me that looking at the truth will only help you. Maybe it would have been all right if none of this had ever come up, but it did. Now, you need the answers to your questions, to set everything straight again."

She felt better, hearing what she instinctively believed put into Matt's words. "Are you always like this?"

"Like what?"

"Sensitive, smart."

For an instant, a look came into his eyes that wasn't sympathy, wasn't the confident kid, wasn't anything she'd seen before. . . .

"Cassidy, I—"

A sharp rap on the passenger-side window interrupted whatever he might have said. Cassidy reacted to the sudden noise by scooting as far across the seat as she could, closer to Matt.

A long-jawed, gap-toothed man stared in at them. "You kids can't park here. This is a loading zone. That's my store." He pointed to the Military Artifacts shop behind him. "I got a shipment coming in, and you're blocking the parking space for the truck."

"Sorry, we're leaving right now," said Matt.

"Kids," muttered the man, and returned to his shop.

Cassidy didn't realize until then how much the unexpected banging on her window had shaken her nerves. She had instinctively moved closer to Matt for protection, and now was embarrassed by her action. "I'm too jumpy," she said, and started to pull away.

"You're trembling." He put his arm around her shoulders. "Stay close."

She didn't know what else to do, so she stayed. And it was comforting, being next to Matt. She felt safer with him, not just that he would protect her from any harm, but that he cared about what happened to her.

Sitting so close to Matt, she didn't think about her mother, or murder, or any of the fears that had troubled her days and nights. She didn't think of anything, allowing herself to drift into a warm sense of peace and comfort. By the time they drove up to the address on Oak Knoll, her trembling had stopped.

There was still a house at this address, an old one, a place a college student might rent. The wood was grayed with age, and the grass was brown from lack of water.

"Doesn't look like much, does it?" she offered.

"Nope. C'mon, let's see if anybody lives here."

They got out, tramped across the dead grass, and climbed the four wooden porch steps. It was going up the steps . . . that action alone, that brought a flash of memory to Cassidy.

"Oh, Lord," she said, the breath caught as if grabbed by a fist in her chest.

"What? What is it?"

"I did this before, these steps; I remember climbing them with my mother. She held my hand. For a second, I could still feel her holding my hand."

"Really? Hey, that's great. It's coming back."

Cassidy nodded, unable to say more. There was something she didn't tell Matt, something she'd heard in her mind at the same instant she'd felt that memory of her mother's hand. It was a voice—a man's voice. He was on the other side of her, walking up the steps, and he'd called her . . . *Button.*

Six

The woman who lived in the house was old, probably in her eighties. Her hair was white, and her forehead, cheeks, sagging chins, and neck were ripples of folded skin and wrinkles. Her back was bent in a dowager's hump, and she shuffled onto the porch with the help of a cane. But her eyes were bright as lake water in the sun, dark blue and shining.

"Who is it you said you're asking about?" Mrs. Cook directed to Cassidy. "You'll have to speak up, dear. I'm a little hard of hearing on this side."

Cassidy didn't want to shout these private questions loud enough for everyone on the block to hear. She stepped closer and practically spoke into Mrs. Cook's ear. "We want to know if you remember a woman who lived here about fourteen years ago. Her name was Anne Logan, and she had a little girl. Were you living here fourteen years ago?"

"Living here? Oh, yes. I've been here forty years—fifteen with my dear husband, Edward, and the last twenty-five years as a widow. Oh, yes," she said again, this time with more sadness in her voice, "I've been here a long, long while."

Cassidy thought they must have the address wrong. How could her mother have lived here, if Mrs. Cook had been here all that time? Disappointed, and ready to give up, she started back down the steps.

It was Matt who asked the right question. "Did you ever rent part of your house to college kids, or other roomers?"

" 'Course I did," said Mrs. Cook. "There was no ordinance against it, not then. Government didn't tell you what you could and couldn't do with your own property in those days."

Matt shared a glance of triumph with Cassidy. "One of those students might have been the woman we're here about, Anne Logan."

"What about her?" asked Mrs. Cook, suspiciously.

Cassidy stepped close again and spoke up. "I want to find out about her, that's all. I'm her daughter."

Mrs. Cook studied Cassidy with a lot more interest. "You're Annie's little girl?"

Cassidy nodded.

"Cassidy, wasn't it? That was Annie's baby, a round-faced, sweet little thing with dark brown hair. I used to hold her on my knee when her mama would go to classes. And you're Annie's child?"

"Yes, I'm Cassidy." It was thrilling to know that someone remembered her, like vivid images from another life drawn from a deep well.

"Well then, you'd better come inside. You'll want to see where you used to live, I expect."

They followed Mrs. Cook through the front door, and into the living room of the house. It was a spacious, shady area, with solid, comfortable-looking furniture, polished plank floors, and white eyelet curtains tied back with ribbons.

"You remember this floor, I'll bet," said Mrs. Cook. "You used to slide around on it in your socks. Your mother always tried to stop you, but I told her there's no stopping a two-year-old who can slide. It's too much fun."

Cassidy wished she could remember this, but she didn't. The eyelet curtains seemed like something she'd seen somewhere, but it might have been in a picture from a magazine, or someone else's house. She didn't feel any certainty that the memory was from this house, or from the time she lived here.

"You come with me now, Cassidy." Mrs. Cook reached for her hand. "There's something I want to show you."

They moved at the old woman's pace, crossing through rooms and barriers of time, all at the speed of frail age. Cassidy tried to look everywhere as they passed, into the cool darkness of a bedroom, along the walls of a large and quaint-with-knickknacks kitchen, and at the old framed photos placed like spirit-mirrors on the walls of the hallway. She wondered, was her mother's face among them?

Mrs. Cook led Cassidy to the outside door at the

back of the house, and to a green yard full of a well-tended vegetable garden and a small orchard of peach trees. "Now, I know you'll remember those trees. You practically lived in that orchard when you were little, playing in the shade of those trees with your toys. Go on," Mrs. Cook urged her. "You step out there and have a look around."

It was the smell of the peach trees that Cassidy remembered, a sweetness that flavored the air with the scent of ripe peaches. She stood beneath the trees and closed her eyes, breathing deeply, wanting to draw the memory into her. And she could remember . . . sitting here as a child, talking to her doll, coloring the pages of a book. It seemed . . . she almost saw her mother's face.

"You do remember being here, don't you?" said Mrs. Cook.

"Yes. You were right. It was these trees that brought it back."

"How could anyone forget them? It's a thing you carry inside you, I guess. Something that makes a place home. My Edward planted our orchard for me when we first came to this house. We didn't have much, but those trees are his legacy to me. He knew how much I loved the taste of fresh peaches."

They had turned around and were heading back to the house when Cassidy saw something else she remembered. It was a wine-colored bougainvillaea, growing on a trellis laid between the bedroom windows, and along the roof line of the house. Seeing it shocked her. Not because it was beautiful. Not because of any remembered scent. But because, in an image as instant as a flash from a camera, she knew she'd seen that bougainvillaea before, and seen her mother standing in front of it with a man.

"Are you all right, dear? Would you like a glass of water?"

"I—I'm fine. I feel a little strange. Could I sit down for a minute?"

"You come inside," said Mrs. Cook, putting an arm around Cassidy's shoulders. "It must be a shock, finding things from so long ago. You sit in this chair in the kitchen. I'll get you a glass of cool water."

"Are you okay?" asked Matt.

"Um-hmm."

"I'd better take you home. Did you remember something?"

"I think so—my mother and a man, standing by that plant at the back of the house. It was so weird. I can remember her in that one second, like the image was burned into my mind."

"Here's your water, dear," said Mrs. Cook. "Take a sip or two. That's right. Are you feeling better?"

"Yes, thank you."

Mrs. Cook sat in the chair beside Cassidy's. "It was a terrible thing that happened to your mother, dying the way she did, and a tragedy for you to get over. I could never imagine anyone wanting to hurt Annie. She was like those peaches out there. Made you feel good about life being around her.

Why anybody would kill someone like dear Annie, I'll never know."

"Do you remember any of the people she knew when she lived here?" asked Matt.

"Oh, not too well. She had one or two girlfriends who would stop by on occasion. I don't recall their names."

"Any men?"

"Matt!" said Cassidy, and glared at him.

"Yes, there was a man in her life. She tried to keep him secret, even from me. But I think I saw him once. It was on the last day of her life."

Cassidy wanted to ask—Who?—but it was as if someone had struck her in her chest with a fist. She barely had air enough to breathe, much less speak.

Matt asked for her. "Who was he?"

"He was a young man, not much older than she. They stood out in the yard and talked for a long time. I was in my kitchen, and I heard him raise his voice. He was angry about something, and I heard him shout, 'I can't believe you'd do that to me!' She came running in the house crying, and he left."

"Where—where was I?" asked Cassidy, feeling the tightness in her chest begin to ease.

"You, dear? Oh, I don't recall. You were around somewhere, I expect."

Mrs. Cook didn't have to tell her. Cassidy knew where she had been . . . sitting in the orchard, beneath the shading branches of the peach trees, watching the man who'd grabbed her mother by the shoulders. His face wasn't clear, but she remembered exactly how she'd felt at that moment—as if her world were coming apart.

And it had.

After Cassidy and Matt left Mrs. Cook's home, they tried the address on Raymond. It turned out to be a restaurant, and the owners knew nothing about any apartment building or house that might have been at the same location years before. Cassidy stood on the sidewalk outside the building and hoped for some sense of recognition of this area from her childhood, but nothing surfaced. Her only connection with this street was the way it looked now, full of upscale shops and restaurants.

"Okay," said Matt, "this was a washout, but finding the other address was a success."

Cassidy knew he was trying to cheer her. "Meeting Mrs. Cook was wonderful. She asked me to come back and visit, and I will. I have so many questions I want to ask her. It never would have happened without your help. I don't know how to say thanks, Matt."

His eyes crinkled at the outside corners, and his lips pulled into a smile. "I do. How about being my date for the prom?"

The invitation was completely unexpected. She wasn't even a senior. There were so many other girls he could have asked, so many who would have said yes. And she did like him, very much, but she wasn't sure about going to the prom. "So much has been happening in my life lately. I don't know if I can stop thinking about it long enough to think about parties and dances. I get kind of down about all this. A prom's supposed to be fun. Bringing me as your date might be a real drag."

He laughed. "We'll talk about it later. For right now, just remember I've asked you, okay?"

"All right."

From that point on, she knew he liked her. She'd known he liked her before, but had tried to tell herself it was just as a friend. Now, she knew Matt wanted them to be something else. Something more. And maybe she did, too. She was definitely attracted to Matt, to his happy eyes and easy smile, and to the way he was so willing to offer his time to help her. But there were a lot of things going on in her life. Right now, her main focus was finding out about her mother. Beyond that, it was hard to know her feelings. Everything was so confused.

They walked back to where the car was parked. Matt opened the door for her, then went around to his side and got in. He put the key in the ignition, started to turn it, then stopped. Instead, he leaned back in his seat and turned his head toward her.

She almost asked him what was wrong, but a glance at his face and the look in his eyes, told her he wanted to kiss her. It wasn't the first time she'd been kissed, but it was the first time she'd wanted to be kissed, by someone she cared about as much as Matt.

He leaned across the seat. His hand reached out

and his fingers touched her face, tilting her head toward his. It didn't happen in a rush, but slowly, gently, with Matt watching her eyes as he neared her. And then her eyes closed, and she felt the warm press of his lips against hers.

Sensations of such intensity rose in her, when the kiss ended and Matt drew back, she almost reached for the door handle of the car, needing to pull away from these strong feelings of emotion and desire.

"Matt, I—"

He must have sensed the panic in her. "It's okay. I shouldn't have pushed. I know you're feeling pretty vulnerable right now."

"It's not that I don't like you," she stammered. "I do."

"You do?"

"Um-hmm."

"Good. That's all I need to know. We've got lots of time. Don't get scared away from me, Cassidy. I'd never do anything to hurt you."

"Okay." She felt more at ease, and a little foolish for reacting the way she had. Matt was her friend. She trusted him, even with the secrets of her life, the emotional struggle within her family, and her mother's murder.

He drove her home. She opened her door. "Matt, you were right about me being scared. I shouldn't have been—not with you—but I was, a little. After the things Dr. Randall told me about slipping into some kind of catatonic trance . . . when I feel myself begin to panic, I worry that maybe it's going to happen again. Can you understand?"

"That's not going to happen, Cassidy. You're all right, now."

"I need you to keep telling me that. Thanks, Matt." She leaned close and brushed his cheek with a kiss.

She got out of the car, started up the walk to the front door of her house, and heard him call out to her, "See you in school tomorrow."

There was something safe and secure in the way she felt about Matt. He was going to help her get through all of this, be there for her, and help find the answers she needed.

Seven

It happened again. She saw the man's hand with the knife. He raised his arm, and the blade of the knife was silvered in the pale cast of moonlight.

Inside her, Cassidy heard the sound of her own scream. "Mama!" But her cry was silent, locked within the walls of her mind. The man with the knife didn't react, or turn toward her. And her mother never heard the warning. The two figures were nearly shadows, silhouettes against a blue-white wash of near dark.

The swing had stopped its motion, the curved seat too high for her to jump down to the soft ground below. Her fingers gripped the side chains. She was afraid she'd fall. Afraid he'd hear. And she didn't want him to see her, didn't want his face to turn into the light and let her see his eyes. Because something was wrong. Mama was crying.

Mama was saying, "Go away, John. Leave me alone." And then she turned to face him.

In that sudden turn, in the muted cast of the moonlight, Cassidy saw her mother's eyes . . . and watched them change from tearful sadness, to stark terror.

The knife plunged into her mother's chest. Cassidy heard it pierce the fabric of the white dress and plunge into yielding flesh. She heard Mama's voice. "Don't—no, don't!"

And then, her mother's glance turned toward her, toward Cassidy on the swing. She said no words, but the look in her eyes was meant for Cassidy alone. In that glance was fear for her child, and something else. Goodbye.

The man pulled back the knife. The blade wasn't silvery now. It was dark with her mother's blood. He stepped closer, into the pooled light, and stabbed the knife into her mother's throat.

Cassidy heard the blade rip across Mama's neck. That sound made her cry out, a single, strangled sob. It rose up from the depths of her and could not be held back.

The man with the knife heard, and turned his head. Looked right at Cassidy. Saw her.

Cassidy woke, the dream still riveting through her. At first she couldn't breathe, her lungs too tight with panic. The room was dark, still night. Had she cried out? Would her parents rush into the room to see if she were okay?

She listened, but there was only silence.

This time, she was alone to face it. Again, she had dreamed of her mother's death. A chill slick of sweat lay on her skin. Fear. Her nightgown smelled of it, the cloying odor of terror. It clung to her, damp in the roots of her hair.

She wouldn't sleep again this night. Switching on the lamp beside the bed, she grabbed her robe and headed for the bathroom and shower. Soap and water would take away the scent of fear.

But what would take it from her mind?

The hot water stung her skin, beating tiny points of warmth against her back and neck. She let it drench her hair, and trickle over her face. The shampoo smelled of apricots. She lathered it in, luxuriating in the pleasant fragrance and the soothing heat.

She rinsed, turned off the stream of water, and stepped onto the bath mat. Cold, predawn air touched her skin. She wrapped herself in the nubby softness of the towel.

There had been more to the dream this time. She didn't want to, but she couldn't help thinking about it. Before, it had always been silent, a mute nightmare, the vision of a tormented child, with silence like a hand stretched across her mouth.

She knew the murdered woman in the dream was her mother, and for the first time, Cassidy had heard her mother's voice. The words were jumbled in her memory. She had to close her eyes and press back into her mind . . . then she heard them again, clearly.

Don't, no don't!

The horror of those words shuddered through her. It was when he'd stabbed her mother, when the knife—

Shivering, Cassidy dropped the damp towel and pulled the robe around her. Don't think about it. Don't remember. Her wet hair snaked cold on her neck. Droplets of water dripped down her back.

She remembered her mother's eyes.

"I don't want to think about it!" The words forced themselves to her lips, as if she couldn't hold back the need to say them aloud. "Oh, please. I don't want to think about it anymore."

But she did think about it, for there was something else her mother had said. It waited at the back of Cassidy's mind, like an unseen stalker hiding in the dark.

She opened the door and padded barefoot back to her room. The light was reassuring, comforting. Light would keep away the nightmare. She climbed back into bed, pulling the robe around her, a covering shield. The pillows were bunched along the headboard. She sat, leaning her back against them.

Maybe her parents were right. Maybe she shouldn't be searching for the answers to her mother's death. What good would it do, except to terrify her? What good had it done so far, the few facts she'd learned?

It had made the nightmare worse. It had made her remember more. Now, she'd heard the fear in her mother's voice. Saw her eyes. And she'd seen the knife, heard the sound of it cutting into her mother's body, tearing across her throat.

Something else surfaced, touching like a cold hand on her brow.

It was 5:00 A.M. Cassidy looked at the clock on her table. She'd have to wait until seven-thirty, until the light of morning, before she could see Rory and Matt at school. She had something important to tell them.

The dream had given her more than she'd realized. It had given her a name. The words were cold whispers in her mind.

Go away, John. Leave me alone.

John. It was the name of her mother's killer.

"What's this?" Cassidy asked.

Matt held a sealed envelope in his hands. "A surprise present from the DMV."

After this morning, she didn't know if she could stand any more surprises. She hadn't told Matt or Rory about the dream. In the crush of people before classes, there'd been too much noise and commotion to concentrate on what she wanted to say to them. Now, it was afternoon, and Matt was holding this envelope like a prize.

"I didn't open the letter," he said, "but I think I know what's in it."

"Go on." Rory seemed as anxious as Matt. "Open it."

Cassidy tore her fingernail under the flap. Inside the envelope were two folded sheets of a letter. It was addressed to Matt from the Department of Motor Vehicles in Sacramento. She read it aloud for Rory and Matt.

"Dear Mr. Austin:

It is not California policy to release personal information, even under the Freedom of Information Act, because of the recently imposed Stalker Law. However, when the application is for information about a deceased person, as you have correctly pointed out, we are allowed to submit the requested material. I have included the electronic abstract of the DMV records, as well as a Xerox copy of Anne Logan's driver's license."

"Matt," said Rory, "you're a genius."

Cassidy thought so, too, and would have said as much, but all her concentration was focused on lifting the first page of the letter, and looking at the one beneath it. The photocopy was a black-and-white Xerox of poor quality, hard to read and grainy. But the thumb-size picture staring back at Cassidy was the image of her mother.

"Jeez," said Matt, leaning over her shoulder. "She looks a lot like you."

"I look like her."

"Yeah, I guess that's right."

Cassidy stared at the blurred Xerox of the photo. It was hard to tell very much, except that Anne Logan had dark hair like Cassidy's, and her face was the same general shape.

"She was pretty," said Matt.

"D'you think so?" Cassidy tried to see prettiness in her mother's face, in her eyes, but all she could imagine was fear.

"She was so young," said Rory. "Not much older than us. It's so sad."

Cassidy reacted to the remark by abruptly folding the papers back into the envelope.

Matt was blunter. "You could go all day without saying stuff like that."

"What? Tell me," demanded Rory. "What did I say?"

"Doesn't matter." Cassidy tried to stop them before they got into it. Rory and Matt were like a squabbling brother and sister, each competing for the bigger share of Cassidy's friendship. She didn't have the energy to deal with them.

The bell rang. Rory grabbed her books and tromped off toward the science wing. "Boy, some people are unbelievably sensitive."

Cassidy picked up her books, too. She put the DMV letter in one of them.

"Don't let what Rory said get to you."

"I'm not. It's okay, really."

"She just doesn't think before she opens her mouth sometimes," said Matt.

"I guess I know Rory pretty well by now. She's my friend. She'd never do anything to hurt me. You were a little hard on her."

His expression showed he realized it. "Yeah, I guess. I'll talk to her later, get things right between us."

"Good. I don't want you two getting mad at each other because of me. If that happens, I'll stop trying to find out about my mother." She glanced away from Matt. "Maybe I should stop anyway."

"Stop? Why? I thought you wanted to know all you could about her. What's going on? Did something else happen?"

"Sort of. I'll tell you about it after school." She started in the direction of her next class, and called over her shoulder, "We'll be late."

Algebra again. It was always algebra when it seemed her world was coming apart. Her mind was so involved with thinking about everything else, it couldn't concentrate on solving polynomial equations, quotients, or coefficient numerical factors.

What she wanted to think about was a knife shimmering in the moonlight, her birth mother's frightened eyes, and a murderer named John.

"What are you studying?" asked Mary Thornton, picking up Cassidy's English textbook. She leafed through the volume absentmindedly.

Cassidy was surprised her mother had voluntarily entered her room. Since the night when her dad had told her about the adoption, her mother had seemed to have avoided any contact with Cassidy. They lived in the same house, but they didn't talk to each other. Her mother openly resented Cassidy's curiosity about her birth mother. Maybe there was more than that, but they hadn't been able to discuss it.

Tonight was the first offer of peace between them. Cassidy sat up, more than willing to do her part. She loved her mother, the woman she'd grown up with, the woman she'd always thought of as her only mother. More than anything, she wanted them to be a close, loving family again.

"We're studying the poems of John Keats," she said. " 'Ode To A Nightingale.' "

"Oh, I always loved that one," said Mary Thornton. A faraway expression transformed her face, and she quoted a line from the poem. " 'Was it a vision, or a waking dream?' "

"That's right," said Cassidy.

Her mother sat on the corner of the bed, still turning the pages of the book. "I know we haven't talked much lately, and I regret that."

"It's okay."

"No, it isn't. Your father and I understand how much of a shock it was for you to find out about your adoption the way you did. That was wrong. Of course you wanted to know about your birth mother all at once, but Cassidy . . ."

An envelope slipped out of the book and fell to the floor.

"What's this?" her mother asked, looking at the return address on the envelope.

"It's nothing." Cassidy tried to reach for the letter, but her mother moved back, opening the folded papers and beginning to read. "That's mine," Cassidy said. "Please give it back to me."

Mary Thornton's hand went to her throat as she read. "My God, do you realize what you're doing? You're letting the killer know you're looking for him. Can't you let it be?"

Now, Cassidy was angry. "How can I when you won't tell me anything?"

Her mother stared at the second page, the one with the picture of Anne Logan. "Oh, Annie. I can't bear to think about all of this again." Tears welled in her mother's eyes. Her arm dropped to her side, the pages of the letter falling to the floor.

Cassidy felt pity and love for her, but couldn't

stop the questions, not now. "You knew her, didn't you?"

"Of course I knew Annie," said her mom. "She was my sister."

Eight

Cassidy hadn't expected anything like this. It was unbelievable. She'd never heard about any relatives on her mother's side of the family. Her grandparents had died before Cassidy was born, and as far as she'd known, her mother had been an only child. It was incredible that her parents had kept this secret from her.

"Will you get me a glass of water, please?" said her mother. "My throat feels so strange and tight."

Cassidy was desperate to hear about this latest revelation, but she noticed her mother did look suddenly pale around her mouth and eyes. "Sit down for a minute, Mom." She helped her to the edge of the bed. "I'll be right back."

Cassidy hurried to the kitchen and drank a few quick sips of cold water herself while she stood at the sink. *Annie Logan was her mom's sister.* That meant her mom, sitting on the bed in Cassidy's room, was really her aunt.

It was too much. She felt like crying.

Her mother had always been there for her, birthday parties and Girl Scouts, taking her to ballet classes and ice-skating lessons. She was her mom—and now, she wasn't.

Somehow, it was harder to accept, because her birth mother and her mom were sisters. That was such a close bond, yet her mom had told Cassidy nothing about the woman who'd given birth to her. Why? Because she'd been killed? Was that enough of a reason?

She carried the glass of water to her room. Her mom was lying on the bed, her face turned toward the wall when Cassidy came through the doorway.

"The water's not very cold. I could get some ice if you—"

Cassidy stopped talking. There was no reaction from her mother. She hadn't turned her head when she heard Cassidy speak, or tried to sit up. She was totally still. Too still.

"Mom?"

No response.

"Mom, are you okay?"

Dead silence was her only answer. *Dead.*

Cassidy touched her mother's arm. The arm slid lifelessly over the side of the bed.

"Dad!" She wanted to run from the room, but she didn't want to leave her mother alone. "Dad!"

She heard his heavy footsteps on the stairs. Running toward her room. "Mary?" Her dad's voice sounded like a stranger's. Not the familiar, confident voice of her father, but like someone else. Frightened. "Cassidy, go downstairs. Call 911."

She couldn't move.

"Cassidy, do it!" her dad shouted.

She ran, taking the treads on the stairs two at a time, pressing the numbers on the phone, too breathless to speak when the emergency dispatcher answered.

"What is your emergency?" asked the annoyingly calm woman's voice on the line.

Cassidy wanted to speak, but it was as if fingers were squeezing tight around her throat. Barely enough space for a thin stream of air to pass through.

"Do you need medical assistance? This is 911. What is your emergency?"

Cassidy could only make choking sounds. Tears of frustration burned in her eyes. She needed a doctor for her mother. An ambulance. *Please, please,* she wanted to beg the woman, *send help.* But the words were locked somewhere between Cassidy's mind and her throat. She couldn't speak.

In complete frustration, she hung up the phone.

"Cassidy," her father shouted, "did you get them? Where is that ambulance?"

The trembling started just above Cassidy's ankles. She felt it climb the calves of her legs to her knees, and travel up, until she couldn't stand. Leaning all her weight against the wall, she slid to the floor, until she sat with knees bent and arms motionless at her sides. It was as if both her voice and body were paralyzed. Just as they'd been when she was little. When she'd seen her birth mother die.

Don't let it be happening again. Fear filled her senses. Fear for her mother, but fear for herself, too. *Please, God.* She had become catatonic once. The doctor said she had slipped into a state of separateness from the rest of the world. Was that happening again? Was it happening now?

No. She fought against her mind's need to shut down her ability to speak and move. That had been her retreat from harm once, the way a two-year-old protected herself from the horrible things she'd seen . . . but Cassidy was older and stronger now. She struggled to stay alert, to feel her senses returning.

Mom needs me. That thought pulled Cassidy back from the dulling, comforting dark. She concentrated on how scared she was, let herself feel the fear, and allowed it to touch her. She hadn't done that before. Not that other time, when she was little. Nothing had touched her then. She hadn't let it.

Now, when she was at her weakest, the images came . . .

She saw the scene again, knew it was coming, and felt the now familiar images overtake her mind. She saw her birth mother, Annie, wearing a white dress and surrounded by filtered shades of green. The park. It was quiet, nearly dark, and from the eyes of memory, the eyes of a two-year-old, Cassidy saw the expression on her mother's face change when she saw the man approach. As Cassidy saw him step out of the shelter of trees and into the pale wash of moonlight where her mother stood.

The silvery knife was in his hand. Cassidy watched

Annie's eyes follow the rise of the man's arm. Eyes rounded with terror. Eyes seeing death approach in the quick thrust of the descending blade. Watched as the knife struck Annie's body . . . blood soaking the white dress . . . and the man stepping into the trembling light.

Or, was it Cassidy who was trembling?

He stepped into the light, pulled the knife back, dark blood dulling the silvery blade, and plunged it now into Annie's throat.

Cassidy felt the muscles of her own throat clench, gripped like a steel vise to protect her from the knife. Remembering, she felt all sense of her body begin to disappear . . . so the blade couldn't touch her. So she couldn't feel the sudden pain of the knife. Pain that echoed in her mother's piercing scream. The scream that ended abruptly in the sharp cut of the blade.

All of it came back. All the feeling of that moment, the sense of terror at witnessing her mother's brutal murder, and the panic that had paralyzed her as a child, when the man turned his face into the light and saw her.

She saw him. He looked right at her, but her mind wouldn't let her remember his face. Some protective shield in her consciousness wouldn't allow her to see the man's face. For when she saw him she would know her mother's killer. She would remember, and when she did, he would come for her. Who would protect her then?

It all returned, the terrible images etched in blood in a child's mind, and the sense of abandonment which came after, when the man left them and went away, and Cassidy was alone.

She fought against sinking into the smothering memory of that fear. Struggled to blink back the images and see the reality that was before her. Right now. Right this moment.

The dreamlike images faded. She stared clearheaded into the living room. And into the intense blue eyes of a stranger.

"Miss, are you all right?"

Cassidy tried to draw back, but the wall stopped her escape. The man was close, kneeling in front of her, his face only inches from her own. *He was inside her house.* He'd followed her from the nightmare memory. He would raise his arm and she'd see the silvery knife . . .

"N-n-n-no!" she screamed, breaking the grip of silence. She tried to get up, to run, but her legs were too weak. *Crawl!* Get away, before he—

"Cassidy, what's wrong? Stop struggling. Let us help you. Look at me, Cassidy. It's John Terrell."

Another set of hands reached for her. Someone else.

"Don't . . . don't!"

"Let her go, Kev," said Terrell. There were two of them, two strangers in her house. "Step back and give her some room."

She saw them clearly now. Two policemen.

"It's all right," said the taller of the two. "You remember me, don't you Cassidy? I'm the officer who picked you up on the night of the accident. John Terrell, remember?"

She looked, and then she did remember. "You went with me to the hospital."

"That's right."

"What are you doing in—why are you here?"

The partner, Kevin, shot a questioning glance at Terrell.

"You called us," said Terrell, "or someone did. Someone from this house dialed 911."

It came back to her in a rush. "My mom! She's upstairs. I tried to call you but I couldn't . . ." She didn't finish the sentence. Tears choked her voice.

"Kev, go upstairs and see about the mother," said Terrell. "I'll stay with Cassidy."

Cassidy wished he had gone with his partner. She didn't want anyone to see her cry. The tears were a kind of release from the rage of not being able to help her mother. "Why couldn't I speak? What's wrong with me? I tried, I really tried, but—"

"Take it easy." He stroked back loose hair that had fallen over her eyes and face. "C'mon, everything's okay. Whatever it is, I'm not going to let anything hurt you, understand?"

She nodded, but she didn't believe.

"Why don't you tell me what's going on." The sound of his voice was calming, soothing.

"I don't know," she cried. "I don't know anything anymore. Maybe I am going crazy. That's what my doctor thinks. That's what my parents think, too. What's wrong with me? What's wrong?"

"Look, I don't know what anyone's been telling

you," he said, "but there's nothing wrong with you, kid. Whatever the problem is, I'm sure—"

"John," called his partner, "better call for an ambulance to transport this lady to the hospital."

"An ambulance," cried Cassidy. She started to get up.

"Sit down and stay put," ordered John Terrell. He headed for the front door to make the call from his car. At the doorway, he turned back to her. "Don't move."

Cassidy stayed put, not because he'd told her to, but because she felt too weak to stand or walk. What if something terrible was wrong with her mom? What if they took her to the hospital and she died?

I can't lose both mothers, thought Cassidy. *If Mom dies, if something I did made this happen . . .*

She heard the wail of the ambulance siren from a few blocks away. The sound grew louder as it neared. Like a child crying. Like the two-year-old child Cassidy had been, still hiding within her mind. Only Cassidy could hear her. Only she could hear the wailing cry, and feel the child's tears that fell unseen. Inside.

The ambulance arrived. John Terrell let the medical attendants into the house. Cassidy saw the team of two men carry their equipment through the living room and up the stairs. Terrell stayed with her.

"Are you feeling better?"

"I don't know what I'm feeling. I'm scared, I know that."

"What are you scared of, Cassidy?"

"I'm scared my mother might die . . . like my birth mother."

"You know about Annie?"

She glanced at him. Something in his voice betrayed John Terrell's interest. "How did you know her name?"

He looked disturbed. "I've said more than I should have. Your father wouldn't thank me for it."

"Never mind what my father would say. Tell me how you knew Annie's name. I'm going crazy trying to figure this out. Why won't anybody talk to me? What's everyone keeping from me?"

"It's just . . . your parents don't like me very much. They don't want me to be involved in your life. They never did. It was because of them that I stayed away I wanted to—"

"Damn you, Terrell. Why are you in my house?"

Cassi had never seen her father look so angry. He was at least twenty years older than John Terrell, but he looked as if he were going to hit him. He stood in the doorway between the hall and the living room.

"Haven't you done enough to this family? I should have made certain we put a stop to you years ago. Understand this once and for all: you're not wanted around this house or this family. I plan to report this incident, and if you come near my daughter again, I'll see that you're arrested. Now, get out!"

"Arrested!" shouted Terrell.

"That's right."

"Come on, John," said Terrell's partner. "Maybe we'd better leave."

"You get him out of here," said her dad. "And you'd better keep him away. If I find him in my house again, around my family, I'll shoot him myself."

Terrell took a step toward him, and Cassidy ran between them, and into her father's arms. "Leave him alone," she yelled at Terrell. "Can't you see he's upset because of my mom? Don't hurt my father."

"The kid's right," said Kevin, Terrell's partner. "Everybody's on edge because the lady upstairs is not feeling so good, huh? Come on, the paramedics have the situation under control. It's time we take off, buddy." He tugged at Terrell's arm, trying to lead him toward the front door.

"I'd be careful who I threaten," Terrell told Cassidy's father. "I've let you have your way all these years, Burke. I'm not sure you're right anymore. Maybe it's time the kid had some answers. Look at her." He glanced at Cassidy. "Don't you see what all this secrecy is doing to her?"

"Get out!" Her dad pushed Cassidy behind him and advanced on Terrell.

"Back off!" Kevin said to Cassidy's father, stepping between the two men. "We're leaving. You'd better calm down, or you'll be dealing with me instead of him. Now back off."

Cassidy's dad stepped back. His face was blood

red, and the veins along his neck stood out like cords.

"C'mon, Dad," she told him. "Let's go to the hospital with Mom."

"The girl's making sense," said Kevin. "You go to the hospital with your wife, and we'll take off. Okay?"

Terrell was staring at Cassidy. The way he looked scared her, as if he might grab her and drag her out of the house.

"Dad, please. Let's go." She took her father's hand.

"Okay, honey." The breath left him in a long sigh. "You're right. We should be thinking about your mother."

Cassi could hear the paramedics coming down the stairs. They were carrying her mother on a stretcher. Beneath the oxygen mask, her mother's face looked too pale.

"I don't want Mom to see you," Cassidy said to John Terrell.

He looked straight at her, as if he had something important to say, wanted to say, but didn't speak. There was an expression in his eyes . . . as if she had hurt him by what she'd said.

"We're coming with you," her dad called to the paramedics.

Cassidy turned to see them carry her mother outside to the waiting ambulance. Her dad started out the door. Everything happened so fast. When she turned back, John Terrell and his partner were gone.

Nine

Matt and Rory met Cassidy in the fourth floor waiting room of the hospital. She'd called them after she got there, when her father went into the room with her mother, and left her to wait in the lounge. The walls of the lounge were unrelieved gray, about as cheerful looking as slabs of concrete. There wasn't even a window to break the monotony. Cassidy had occupied herself for the last two hours by counting holes in one of the acoustic tiles above her head.

"How's your mom?" asked Rory.

"I don't know yet. Nobody's telling me anything."

"What's wrong with her?" asked Matt.

"My dad said she might have suffered a stroke, or it could have been her heart."

"I didn't know your mom had a heart condition," said Rory.

"Neither did I," said Cassidy, "until today. I guess she kept it a secret. She kept a lot of secrets."

"Isn't she too young for a stroke or a heart attack?" asked Matt. "I thought most people with those kinds of health problems were in their fifties and sixties."

"My mom's fifty-eight. She was twenty when my birth mother was born."

"Whoa," said Rory, "she's almost my grandmother's age."

"I didn't know you still had a grandmother," said Cassidy.

"I don't. She died two years ago—heart attack."

"You're full of good news, aren't you," Matt said to Rory.

"I didn't mean anything by it. You think I'd deliberately say anything to upset Cassidy right now? I'm not that mean, or that stupid."

"Maybe if you tried to think before you open your mouth—"

"Did you two come here to fight with each other? I mean it," said Cassidy. "If you're going to do this, just go home."

"I'm sorry, Cassi," said Rory. "I came here to help you."

"Me, too," said Matt. "I promise, no more arguments."

"Good, but I'll believe that when I see it."

They sat on a padded bench near the hallway, so Cassidy could see anyone coming out of her mother's room.

"Why won't they tell me what's going on?"

"They're probably busy," said Matt. "You know, they've got to monitor all those machines in the rooms on the critical care floor."

"Critical care? Is that what this is?"

"Yeah," said Matt, "didn't you know?"

"No. That means she's in serious condition, doesn't it?"

Matt didn't deny the truth. "I guess. But hey, this is where they can help her. My dad was on this floor once."

"He was?" It gave her hope. Matt's dad was still around.

"It was his gallbladder. It was infected, I guess, and almost burst. He was starting to get peritonitis. I thought he was going to die. He had emergency surgery, and they brought him to the fourth floor afterward to recuperate."

"That must have been scary," said Cassidy. "Were you waiting here all by yourself?"

"Yeah, most of the time. My mom stayed with him as much as she could for the first couple of days. I got to know this area real well."

"That's so sad," said Rory. "Did I know you then?"

"No. I didn't know anybody. We'd just moved into town."

Cassidy reached over and took Matt's hand. "I wish I could have been there for you."

"Thanks. It wasn't such a big deal. He's fine now. The point is, this is the place you want your mom to be, so they can take care of her. Right?"

"Right."

Rory put her arm around Cassidy's shoulders and squeezed in a wide-angle hug. It was better with these friends here, Matt holding her hand,

and Rory squashing her shoulder blades until they ached.

"I've been wondering. . . . Do you think it's my fault?"

"What?" asked Matt.

"That Mom's here. I mean, she didn't want me to find out about my birth mother, and I kept searching for more information. What if she dies, Matt? Will it be my fault?"

"You can't think that. What were you supposed to do when they told you about being adopted, and that your birth mother was murdered?—pretend you didn't hear it? I would have done the same thing."

"Really?"

"Absolutely."

"Me, too," said Rory. "You haven't done anything wrong. Your mom just got sick, that's all."

Cassidy let out a deep breath. "I'm glad you two are here."

Nobody said much for a while. Conversation seemed insignificant, under the circumstances. Cassidy didn't need her friends to talk. She simply needed them to be with her.

Matt was the one to spot her dad coming out of the room. "Look," he said.

The expression on her dad's face was grim. Cassidy was afraid to ask him how her mother was, but she had to know. She left Matt and Rory on the bench in the visitor's lounge, and walked to meet her father.

"Dad, is she—"

"She's all right, thank God. The doctor says she suffered a mild coronary."

"A heart attack!"

"A very minor one, Cassidy. The doctor says there was minimal damage to the muscle. She should be back on her feet after a few days rest."

"Did I cause it? Was it because of me?"

"No, honey. This is a long-term development. Your mother has known she's had a heart condition for several years."

"Why didn't she ever tell me?"

"She didn't want to worry you. As for today's problem, I think it's more the stress of her job than anything to do with you."

Cassidy wasn't so sure, but she was glad to hear her father say it, anyway. "When can she come home?"

"Not for two or three days. They want her to rest, and there are a few tests they want to run, just to be sure everything's okay. She should be able to come home later this week."

Cassidy wanted to bring her mom home right then. She wanted to take care of her and see with her own eyes that her mom was okay. "Will they let me visit her?"

"Not now. She's on medication to make her sleep. Besides, you're not eighteen. The CCU has strict rules, I'm afraid. They have to be careful of infection."

She was offended. "I'm not a little kid. It's not like I'm going to give her chicken pox, or something."

"I know that, sweetie. These are their rules, not mine. Try to be patient. You'll see her in a few days."

A few days seemed like forever. "Are you sure she's okay? You wouldn't lie to me, would you?"

"No, I swear. Relax, honey. I was scared, too, but the doctor says it was a very minor incident. We were lucky this time."

"This time?" The words left an ominous feeling.

"You mom will have to make some changes in her life-style. Cut back on her work hours, that sort of thing. You and I, we're going to have to make things easier on her for a while. I'm going to have to be here with your mother for the next couple of days. I won't be around home much. Do you think you can manage on your own for that long? Can I count on you for that?"

Cassidy nodded, grateful to have some definite thing she could do to help. Not only could her dad count on her, she was going to make sure her mom didn't do any work around the house when she came home. Cassidy was going to clean, and cook, and—

"So, what did he say?" asked Rory.

Cassidy's dad had gone back into CCU to be with her mom. Now that he was gone, Matt and Rory joined her and listened while she filled them in on all the details.

"That's better than you thought," said Matt. "It's good news."

It was hard to imagine her mother's being hospitalized as good news, but she saw that Matt was right. The doctor's diagnosis could have been a lot worse.

"And, from what you're telling me," he went on, "it sounds as if your mom has had this condition for a long time—which means it wasn't caused by something you did. You can forget about all that guilt."

Could she? Maybe. Or maybe the news about her mom's history of a heart condition only lessened Cassidy's sense of guilt. She knew that some of the stress her mom was dealing with was because of the way Cassidy had reacted to finding out about the adoption, and her birth mother's murder. No matter what anyone said, she carried the weight of that on her conscience. She *was* partly responsible for what had happened today, and she knew it.

They left the hospital, Cassidy, Matt, and Rory. There was no special rush about getting home. Matt's and Rory's folks knew where they were, and no one was going to bug Cassidy about what time she got in. Not today, anyhow.

"Want to get something to eat?" suggested Rory. She was always ready to go out to eat.

"Maybe a public restaurant isn't where she wants to be right now," said Matt.

"Actually, it sounds good." Cassidy hadn't realized until this moment that she was so hungry. "Something not too complicated. You know, comfort food."

"Comfort food?" Rory had obviously never heard the term.

"Stuff your mom used to make when you were little," explained Cassidy. "Creamed tuna on toast, spaghetti, hot dogs, grilled cheese sandwiches."

"Peanut butter and jelly sandwiches with the crusts cut off," added Matt. "Or pancakes."

"Yeah," said Rory, "pancakes."

They wound up at The International House of Pancakes. Cassidy ordered a stack of hotcakes and sausage, Rory had paper-thin orange crepes, and Matt finished two Belgian waffles. Afterward, they sat around the table as full and lazy as three well-fed cats.

"So, what do we do now?" asked Rory.

"We could go to my house, I guess," said Cassidy. "At least we'd have it to ourselves."

Matt stood. "Sounds like a deal. Let's go."

Cassidy had been alone in her house lots of times, but now, even with Matt and Rory there, the place seemed too quiet, too empty. Or maybe it was full of ghosts . . . her mother's, and the ghostlike memory of the killer. How would it be when Rory and Matt left?

"You know," said Matt, "before all the excitement over your mother, you said you were going to tell us something."

"I did?"

"Matt's right," said Rory. "Remember, at school?"

Now she remembered. She had wanted to tell them about the dream, about remembering the killer's name.

"I don't remember," she said. Somehow, it didn't seem right to be talking about it. Not with her mother in the hospital. Not when it was the stress from hearing this kind of stuff that might be what put her mom there.

"Are you sure?" asked Matt. "Whatever it was, we could talk about it."

"I said I don't remember. Why doesn't anybody ever listen to me? Maybe I don't want to remember; did either one of you ever think of that?"

"Cassidy," said Rory, "don't bite our heads off. We're only trying to help you."

"I don't want any help. I'm tired. I don't want to talk to anybody."

"She's right," said Matt. He got up and grabbed Rory by the arm. "We're gonna go home and let you get some rest. We're all tired. I could use some sleep, too."

"I'm sorry," Cassidy tried to tell them. She knew she'd hurt their feelings with her outburst, but she couldn't help it. Her nerves felt as if they were exposed on the surface of her skin. Everything anybody said was like taking sandpaper to those nerves.

"Are you sure you don't want to sleep at my house tonight?" asked Rory. "Won't it be kind of spooky here, all by yourself? My mom wouldn't mind."

"Thanks, but I'll be okay. I think I need some time alone."

"Really?" Rory's eyebrows lifted. "I sure wouldn't, not if some killer was looking for me."

"C'mon," said Matt, and jerked Rory none too gently by the arm. He hustled Rory outside, then turned back from the steps and said to Cassidy, "Call if you need something. Promise?"

"I promise. And thanks."

She watched them drive away, then closed the door. Now she was alone . . . with the house, with her memories, and with the frightening thought Rory had put in her mind: the killer was looking for her.

Ten

Cassidy's dad came home for thirty minutes the next morning, long enough to shower, shave, grab a bite of cold Danish from the fridge, and rush to the office. The hospital had allowed him to stay all night, letting him come in and sit beside her mom for a few minutes every couple of hours.

Cassidy had barely had a chance to speak to him. "Is Mom better?" she'd asked.

"She's awake, pretty groggy because they're keeping her sedated."

"Why are they doing that?"

"For the pain."

Cassidy hadn't thought about her mom being in pain. That was awful. Her mom didn't deserve that. She was so good to everybody. It wasn't right that she should be suffering.

"But, she's going to be okay, isn't she?"

"It looks like she's going to be fine, honey. I wish I could stay and talk to you, but I'm late for work. Are you all right?"

She wasn't. "Sure, I'm fine."

"Good. That's a worry off my mind." He grabbed his coat from the rack by the door. "Oh, I nearly forgot. Don't forget your appointment with Dr. Randall this afternoon."

She had hoped he wouldn't remember. "Why don't I skip it? I don't think he's really helping me. Besides, how would I get there? You're going to be busy."

"Take your mother's car. She won't need it for a few days. In fact, take her car to school. That way, you can drive to his office right after class."

By the change of expression in her father's eyes, she knew her disappointment showed. "It's important that you see him, Cassidy. Please, do it for me, and for your mother. Will you?"

When he put it that way, she couldn't say no.

Dread of seeing Dr. Randall again hung over Cassidy's head all morning during school. By lunch break, she was obsessed with it, worrying herself into such a state, she couldn't eat anything.

"What's the big deal?" asked Rory. "You talk to him a little, he acts interested, and you go home."

"I wish he were only acting interested." Cassidy was pretty sure Dr. Randall was interested. Very. "He's like . . . intense, you know?"

Rory shrugged. "Maybe he's a family friend, like your dad said. It's probably only that. Don't let it get to you so much."

"Yeah, you're right." Cassidy didn't want to talk about him anymore. Thinking about him was bad enough, talking about him was a lot worse.

Matt didn't join them for lunch. Cassidy missed

him. After last night, he probably thought she didn't want to see him at all, but she did. Especially today. She could have used some of Matt's contagious nerve, and his sense of humor.

The hours passed too quickly. In spite of her trying desperately to hold back time, the hour for her appointment came due, like a bill that needed paying. That's how it felt, like a bad debt. She was trying to make it right.

She drove to the psychiatrist's office, wondering what she should tell him. She'd mention her mother's coronary, of course, but wasn't sure she'd tell him about her strange dream, or the bits and pieces of memory that were coming back to her about her birth mother's death. Unless he asked her, she wouldn't bring it up.

"What have you remembered, Cassidy?" It was the first question Dr. Randall asked.

She'd arrived at his office a few minutes early, but was shown in right away. If anything, Dr. Randall seemed more determined than ever to discover what was troubling her. The expression in his eyes was intimidating. She wished her father were in the next room, or better yet, that she weren't here at all.

"You have remembered more about your mother's death, haven't you, Cassidy?"

How did he know? "Only bits and pieces." She didn't want to tell him details. Already, he was making her feel uncomfortable, and she'd only been in the room five minutes. What would it be like after an hour?

"Why do you think I want to know about this?" he asked, surprising her.

"I don't know."

"Do you think it helps me, somehow? Am I the one who's having nightmares about your mother's death?"

"No, of course not."

"'Of course not,'" he mimicked her voice. "Then why are you keeping this a secret from me? I'm trying to help you, Cassidy. Don't you understand that? If you don't tell me what you're remembering, all of it, every detail, then I can't help you to get through this. Do you want to wind up like you were before?"

"You mean, when I was little?"

"Yes, that's what I mean." He seemed angry. "What you're experiencing is very traumatic, reliving a long-suppressed nightmare. That, and the added stress of your mother's being in the hospital. I don't want this to push you over the edge. You have to trust me. I know what's best for you at this moment. I brought you back from numbing depression once. This time, it could be much harder to bring you out of it."

He was scaring her. "You think I'm that close to a breakdown?"

"If I weren't very concerned about you, I wouldn't be pushing you so hard. You must tell me what you're remembering. If you don't, I'm afraid . . ."

"You're afraid, what?"

His expression was threatening. "I don't want to do it, Cassidy, but if you force my hand, I'll see that you're put in a psychiatric hospital for a period of observation."

"What!" She hadn't expected anything like this.

"Believe me, that isn't what I want to do. I'm a friend of your family. The last thing I want is to upset your mother and father any more than they already are, but I won't stand by and let you slip into a serious mental state that may be impossible to penetrate. The fact that you're having flashbacks is an indication that your defenses are down. Trying to handle it by yourself is extremely dangerous."

He couldn't have scared her more if he'd told her the killer was right there in the room with them. Insanity terrified her. That was what he was saying, that she might be slipping over the edge of reason. That she was experiencing a breakdown. Back into the silence.

"What do I do?" she asked, afraid.

"Talk to me."

She told him about the dreams. Her words flowed like the memories, some sentences making sense, others seeming disjointed and fragmentary, like the momentary glimpses of scenes from her childhood. He didn't interrupt, listening as she said it all.

"I saw him," she said, "the man who killed my mother. He stepped into the moonlight, and I saw his face."

"Did you?"

"Yes, but I can't remember exactly. It's as if there's something keeping me from remembering his face. I see it all so clearly: my mother, the man with the knife, the blood, and the look in her eyes when she's dying, but . . ."

"What, Cassidy?"

"Why can't I remember his face?"

"I think you will. Everything you've told me says that you will. It's the thing you're most afraid of, that's why it's still hidden. Your mind won't release the image."

"I might have already seen his face," she volunteered. Her hands were shaking.

Dr. Randall leaned closer. "You think you've seen him somewhere?"

"Yes, maybe . . . I don't know for sure." Her fingers twisted the fabric of her thin, cotton sleeve.

"You could identify him?"

"It was only a glimpse. Not enough to describe anyone."

"What did you see? And where?"

"I was in the backyard of the house where I used to live with my mother—my birth mother," she corrected herself. "I looked toward the house, and remembered seeing Annie," she settled on calling her that, "standing near the bougainvillaea. A man was with her."

"I want you to try to remember him. What did he look like?"

"I don't know. It was only for an instant."

"Was he as tall as I am?"

"Maybe." She tried to turn away from Dr. Randall, but he turned her swivel chair back to face him.

"Look at me and answer my questions. Did he have dark hair like mine, or light?"

"What difference does it make?"

"It might make a very great difference. Think. What do you remember about the way the man looked?"

She knew he was tall, maybe not as tall as Dr. Randall, but it was hard to judge. And his hair was brown. But there was something she remembered much more specifically. He'd looked angry. He and Annie had been arguing, loudly. That's what had made her look up and see him. And for that moment, he had looked right at her. He had—

Cassidy gasped.

"What is it?" Dr. Randall gripped her arm.

She pulled away from him. "Leave me alone. I don't want to talk anymore."

"You've remembered something, haven't you?"

She stood and started for the door. "I'm going home."

He reached for her arm again, but she slipped away from his grasp. "Sit down, Cassidy! I'm your doctor, and I'm telling you, don't leave like this. I can see that you've remembered something. You must not keep it to yourself. Do you hear me?" he called after her as she rushed out the door and through his office waiting room. And then, his final words. "It isn't safe."

That was what she heard over and over in her mind as she hurried to the elevator, as she jabbed the *lobby* button repeatedly, and felt the loud hum of nervousness and rising blood pressure make her head feel like a surging ocean between her ears.

Dr. Randall was right. Cassidy had remembered . . . Annie standing in the garden with a man, arguing. Only now she'd seen his face and knew his identity. She should have realized before. Annie had said the name. "Go away, John. Leave me alone."

John. The face of the man in the garden was sixteen years younger, but she recognized him. He was the same. *Officer John Terrell.*

The house was ghostly with silence when Cassidy came home. No one there to greet her, and no one moving through the too still rooms. The twilight sky was glazed with vivid streaks of rose, orchid, and amber. Inside the house, the rooms were shadowy and cold.

There was a message on the answering machine from her father. He was going to the hospital after work. Her mother was better, he said, but he wanted to stay with her tonight, if possible. "Maybe Rory could come by," he suggested, "or you could spend the night at her house."

Alone again.

Maybe it was better. She needed to think about what had happened. If her dad had been home, she would have told him everything. But he had enough to worry about with her mom's heart problems. And he might have mentioned it to her mother. That was the last thing she wanted to do, make anything worse for her mom.

No, she wouldn't say anything about this—at least, not to her parents.

A door slammed.

"Who's there?" She felt the humming in her ears again, the pounding in her temples. "Dad? Are you home?"

No answer.

The sound had come from upstairs. Maybe he had come home and hadn't heard her. But his car wasn't in the driveway. Who else would be in the house? Who else? The possibility was too scary to think about.

Who knew she'd be here alone? She mentally went through the list of people who knew her mother was in the hospital. Her father, of course, Matt, Rory, Dr. Randall. And John Terrell. He had been in the house on the night of her mother's heart attack. He had responded to the 911 call.

"He's not here. Not here," she said to herself as she climbed the steps of the staircase. He wasn't. Couldn't be. But she had to know, had to be sure.

What if John Terrell had killed Annie? What if he had come back now to kill the only witness to the murder? *I shouldn't be doing this,* she thought. *I should leave the house right now. Get out before something—*

The door slammed again, a loud bang that shook the stairs, and she nearly screamed.

She ran to the room, ran because if she didn't

race upstairs right then and see what it was, she would run out of the house and never come back.

Cassidy's bedroom door was standing open. She was breathing so hard, at first she didn't notice the breeze coming through the window. The curtains were moving; that's what made her see it and realize.

I shut that window. She was sure. Last night, when the house seemed so empty and she'd felt completely unprotected and vulnerable, she had shut the bedroom window and locked it. And now the wind was blowing through. The wind had made the door slam. Like the slamming of her heart.

Someone had been here, in this room.

She stepped across the threshold, checked behind the door, and quickly scanned the room. There was no one. It was hard to hear anything over the sound of her own ragged breathing, so she held her breath and listened. Was she really alone? Was there someone behind the closet door? Or would a hand snake out to grab her ankle from under the bed?

She switched on the overhead light. Then, with a courage that was born of fear, she checked the room, looking under and behind everything, around every corner. Only when she was sure she was alone did she close and latch the window and lock her bedroom door from the inside.

She glanced around. Nothing looked disturbed. Nothing was missing. Her room looked just as she had left it. There wasn't anything of great value in her room that anyone would want to take.

The thought, when it came to her, was sudden and throbbing with uneasiness. She yanked open the bottom drawer of her dresser, flung the folded sweaters and winter gloves onto the floor, and frantically shuffled through the papers hidden beneath the clothes.

It was a small cache of secret belongings, a copy of the microfiche abstract of her birth certificate, the two Xeroxed reproductions of voter registration cards, and the envelope and letter from the DMV.

Anyone else might not have noticed. It didn't look as if anything were gone . . . but Cassidy instantly saw what was missing. The grainy black-and-white photocopy of Annie Logan's driver's license—the one with Cassidy's only picture of her birth mother—had disappeared.

Eleven

"Who would want a crummy DMV picture?" Matt leaned his hands against the window frame and stared outside, as if he might see the answer in the dark.

His hair had been cut that afternoon. It was tapered into clean lines. Cassidy noticed the muscles running along the sides of his neck—straight, sleek, and smooth. The clingy fabric of Matt's shirt clung to him when he leaned forward, and she noticed the broader muscles along his back. The thought came to her to reach out and lay her hand across his neck, but he might think it was a caress. It wouldn't be. It would only be a touch. . . . She kept her hand to herself.

Rory and Matt had come over as soon as Cassidy called them. Matt was acting like some kind of amateur detective, looking around her room and the rest of the house as if he could find clues to the intruder's identity. Rory, on the other hand, was there strictly as a friend, to commiserate.

"Maybe it was the same person," Rory suggested.

"What same person?"

"The one who killed your mother."

"Oh, that's good. Why don't you think of something else to really scare her." Matt turned away from the window and walked back to the bed where Rory and Cassidy sat huddled like bookends. He took Cassidy's hand and pulled, leading her away from Rory.

"Hey, I'm sorry if what I'm saying scares her, but maybe it's true. It's not like what happened is going to go away if you close your eyes and don't think about it. Maybe someone knows Cassidy has been looking into her mother's records."

"Who would know?" Matt shot back. There was anger shining from his eyes. "You've got a real ability to always say the wrong thing at the wrong time."

"I think she needs to hear it!" yelled Rory, whose face had reddened with righteous indignation of her own.

"Cut it out," Cassidy told them. "C'mon, you two, you're my friends, remember? I want to hear what both of you have to say, but don't fight, please. I'm shook-up enough without having to break up arguments between you two."

Matt stared hard at a blank place on the wall. Rory scrutinized her kneecap.

"Let's go downstairs and make a sandwich," Cassidy suggested. They followed her without comment.

The kitchen was wide and full of windows that let in the dark eyes of night. Alone, Cassidy would have been uncomfortable with such vulnerability, but with Matt and Rory beside her, she could look out at the glazed black and think it beautiful. Night covered sadness in the world. It had its own beauty.

She made three grilled cheese sandwiches on the griddle. Cooking calmed her nerves a little. It was normal, when everything else in her life was turned upside down. They ate their sandwiches in silence. By the time there were only crumbs on the plates, whatever anger Matt and Rory had been feeling toward each other was gone.

Rory was the first to come back to the problem. "Are you going to tell your dad about this?"

"No."

"Why not? I don't think you're taking this seriously enough, Cassidy. I don't care what Matt says."

"For once, I agree with you." Matt pushed his chair back from the table. "This isn't a game anymore."

"It never was a game," said Rory, too sharply. "Sorry," she offered, responding to Cassidy's warning glance.

"Keeping this a secret doesn't make sense," said Matt. "If somebody really did break into the house today—"

"Look," said Cassidy, "I'm not telling my dad because he's got enough to worry about right now. He doesn't need any more trouble. Can't you understand that?"

"Okay," Matt conceded, "then if not your dad, what about telling the psychiatrist? Shouldn't he know what's going on?"

SOMEONE'S WATCHING

"Maybe." She didn't know how to tell them she was afraid of Dr. Randall. He'd scared her today with his threats of keeping her in a hospital for observation—a mental hospital. She hadn't said anything to Matt or Rory about that. She was too embarrassed.

"Why don't you call the police and report a break-in?" asked Rory.

"I can't do that."

"Why not?" Rory was the voice of exasperation. "I don't get it."

The police were the last people Cassidy wanted to call. When she'd dialed 911 for her mother, John Terrell had come to her house. After what she'd remembered this afternoon, she was afraid he might be the one who'd killed Annie Logan.

There were very few people who might believe her story. How could she claim to remember anyone's face so clearly? She'd been only two when the murder happened. Until recently, she hadn't remembered it at all. Now, the images were coming together like pieces of a puzzle. She knew what she was remembering was real, and not her imagination.

"If I tell you something," she said to both of them, "will you promise to keep it to yourselves?"

Matt and Rory glanced at each other. Both nodded.

"Okay, but don't start freaking out when I tell you what I remembered."

They waited.

"I think I know who killed Annie."

"Oh, *man,*" said Matt.

Rory's reaction was less subdued. "Are you going to tell us, or drive me crazy? Who?"

Cassidy's voice was nearly swallowed up with nervousness when she said it. "The cop, Officer John Terrell."

"A policeman would have access to all of Annie Logan's records," said Matt. He had listened to everything Cassidy told them about the images and phrases she remembered. To his credit, he hadn't said she was nuts.

"Then why would he want the DMV report?" asked Rory. "If he could get it on his own, why would he take our copy?"

"If it wasn't for him," said Cassidy, "maybe he just didn't want me to have it."

"But, why?" Rory seemed personally aggravated by the very idea. "It doesn't make any sense."

"No, it doesn't." Cassidy's feelings were so confused about John Terrell. When she'd first met him, after the car accident, she hadn't liked the way he'd bullied her. And her parents resented him for something; that was obvious. But when he'd come to the house the last time, when she'd dialed 911, he'd acted so nice.

It didn't seem possible that Terrell could be the one who'd killed Annie, but Cassidy's memories didn't lie. Annie had said his name, right before she was murdered. And the memory was vivid of them arguing in the backyard of the house where she'd lived.

"I still think you should go to the police," said Rory. "Tell them what you've figured out. Let them handle it."

"We don't have any proof of his guilt," said Matt.

Cassidy hadn't considered that. What if she became positive that John Terrell was the man who murdered Annie, but the police wouldn't believe her? Where was the proof? Her memory? She could be sure of it—know it—and he could still walk free.

"You have to be careful," said Matt. "If you accuse him, and then can't prove his guilt in court, he'll know you're dangerous to him. Cops have a way of getting around the law."

That thought chilled her. He'd be the one who was dangerous. How dangerous could a murderer be?

Rory rubbed her arms. "This is creeping me out. I don't think you should stay here alone tonight, Cass. It's not safe. Jeez, the way I'm feeling, it's not safe to be here right now."

"You're okay. There's three of us," said Matt.

Cassidy wasn't so sure. She felt threatened and vulnerable. Someone had been in her house, in her room. Rory was right. She wouldn't sleep at all if she stayed here alone. She'd be listening for every sound.

"Could I stay over with you?"

"My room's got your name on the door."

That was true. When they were twelve, she and Rory had put a small brass plaque on the crosspiece of the door to Rory's room. That summer, it seemed as if Cassidy had lived at Rory's house as much as her own. Things hadn't changed much over the years. She still spent a lot of time with Rory and her family.

"I'd say you guys are a little too chummy," said Matt, making a face about the names on the door.

Rory elbowed him in the ribs.

Cassidy was glad Matt and Rory were with her. They were acting normal, and her life was anything but that. They kept her balanced. Without her friends, she might be slipping over the edge of fear. Dr. Randall had said—

No. She didn't want to think about that.

She left a note for her dad in case he came home, telling him she'd be at Rory's. Once she made up her mind, it didn't take long to get her things and get out of the house. They piled into Matt's car, and took off without looking back. Cassidy was afraid to look . . . afraid of what she might see. Was someone watching?

Even at Rory's, Cassidy couldn't sleep. That night, after they'd talked for hours and Rory finally drifted off to a gentle snoring, Cassidy lay wide awake. It was as if all the muscles in her body were tensed, ready for something to happen. Her nerves were sensitive to everything. Even the sheet touching her skin disturbed her.

The clock said it was 3:00 A.M., but time didn't seem to tick by in the usual way. She had lain awake watching the face of the clock. The hands barely moved. Before this, time had always gone so fast. Now it seemed to crawl.

She got up and went to the window. The night was heavy with dark. There was barely a sliver of moon. It was overcast with a promise of rain, and the clouds obscured even the glittering light of the stars.

Staring into the dark, a sadness welled inside her. She thought of her mother in the hospital. Would she be all right? It was cruel to keep them apart. Cassidy needed her mother now. But her mother wasn't strong enough. She'd had too much pressure, too much strain, in the last few weeks. It had nearly cost her life. Maybe it was better for her mother that they were apart. In the hospital, she could rest and not worry about Cassidy, not try to read the dark thoughts that were going on in her daughter's mind.

She gazed higher into the heavens. Was her other mother watching over her tonight? Was Annie Logan somehow protecting her only child? It seemed possible that she was. The thought filled Cassidy with a peaceful feeling.

"Mother," she whispered, trying the familiar name on a new image—one that she'd tried to forget after Annie's death. It wasn't as if Annie had willingly given her up for adoption, or walked out of her life. Annie's life had been taken from her, and the mother Cassidy had known had been stolen away.

"Mother, watch over me." Tears formed in her eyes and slid without sound down her cheeks.

Tonight, she was so alone, even here, snug in the warmth of Rory's friendship. Her family had been kind and generous, but they were Rory's family, not Cassidy's. Tonight, it was as if everyone who was hers had been taken away: Annie, her mother in the hospital, and even her dad.

Tears blinded her. She bent her head and rubbed her eyes clear. When she opened them again, she saw something that startled her. Outside, parked on the opposite side of the street, about three houses down, was a black-and-white patrol car. Police.

It was John Terrell. She knew it. He had followed her to this house. Could he see her standing in the window? She stepped back, still able to see his car, but hoping he couldn't see her.

The nerve endings of her skin had known this. The muscles of her body had felt it coming. Shock shuddered through her and she wanted to cry out, "What do you want from me? Why are you there?"

She knew the answer. Someone was watching. Not her dead mother's spirit from the world beyond this one, but the eyes of a killer. He was there to be sure she didn't find out too much, enough to incriminate him. He would silence her before that happened—the same way he'd silenced her mother.

Someone was watching, and seeing with the eyes of death.

Twelve

"Is everything okay, Cassidy?"

"Sure, I'm fine."

Her dad was only home long enough to shower and change clothes before he had to go to work. He'd slept at the hospital again. Cassidy had come home to pick up her schoolbooks and some clothes for the next couple of days. By chance, they'd run into each other.

"You look wrung out and hung up wet," he told her.

"What?"

They laughed at the old expression. Laughter sounded good. It drove away some of the gloominess that had settled on the house, and in Cassidy's thoughts.

"I'm not getting a lot of sleep, I guess," she admitted.

"You and Rory staying up late, are you?"

She didn't want to lie to him, but in this case, a lie was better than the truth. "We always keep each other awake; it's a rule."

"Um-hmm, that's what I thought. I won't complain about you staying with her. It's a relief to know you're not here all alone, but try to get some sleep, too."

"Don't worry about me, Dad. I'm young, remember?"

He smiled. "I remember being young, vaguely."

They talked about her mom. She was making a good recovery. The doctor might be releasing her from the hospital the day after tomorrow. She'd have to stay home from work for another two weeks—and then return only part-time—but she was much stronger already.

"She asks me a million questions about you. 'Is Cassidy getting enough to eat? Does she need money for school? How is she handling this emotionally?' I keep telling her you're fine. You are, aren't you?"

That almost made her cry, that her mother was lying in a hospital bed, recovering from a heart attack, and worrying about her. "I'm absolutely okay. Really. Tell Mom I miss her, will you?"

"I will. She loves you very much, Cassi. And so do I."

Now, she did cry. She couldn't stop the tears from spilling from her eyes and down her cheeks. Sobs choked in her throat, and she sounded as if she were hiccupping.

"There is something wrong." Dad held her away from him to look into her eyes. "Have you been having more nightmares? Is that it?"

She didn't know what to tell him. Nightmares seemed a better choice than what she'd really been living through. Nightmares didn't hurt people.

They didn't sneak into a room and steal belongings. Or fill your waking hours with fear. Compared to real life, nightmares were easy.

"Maybe that's why I haven't been sleeping so great," she told him.

"You kept that appointment with Dr. Randall?"

She nodded.

"Good. I hope you're telling him all of this, Cassidy."

She glanced away, unwilling to meet her father's eyes. A lie in words was bad enough, but the truth was harder to hide from her eyes.

"He needs to know about this, honey. I'm going to call him and set up another appointment for you today."

"Dad, no. I don't want to go there again."

"I'm afraid Stewart will insist on it, especially if he knows the nightmares are back. You stay right here while I go phone him. I'll let you know what time to stop by his office."

"Dad," she called after him, but he left the room. A minute later she heard him on the phone to Dr. Randall.

"Yes, I'll tell her. She'll be at your office right after school. Thank you, Stewart. You'll never know how much this means to me. With everything that's happened to Mary, I can't stand being worried about Cassidy right now. I feel like I'm at the breaking point, too. You'll help her, won't you? I've trusted my little girl to you before, and now I have to do it again."

Cassidy felt as if a net were closing in around

her. It was hard to breathe. Her father was making it impossible for her to say no, to refuse to see Dr. Randall. His voice had broken when he was talking on the phone. He'd sounded close to tears. How could she push him past that? And saying no would push him over the edge.

They were all just barely hanging on, her mom, her dad, and Cassidy herself. Maybe seeing Dr. Randall wasn't such a terrible idea after all. By the time her dad came back into the room, she had resigned herself to it.

"You'll do this for me, won't you, Cassi?"

"Sure, Dad."

He didn't smile. Maybe there weren't any smiles left in him, but she knew he was relieved by her answer. He glanced at his watch. "I'm late for work." He leaned over and kissed her on the forehead. "That's from your mother." Then he kissed her on the cheek. "That's from me."

When he left, she felt like all the air in the room had gone with him. She waited until he drove away, then rushed out of the house. Only outside did she feel safe. The idea of being in the house alone scared her worse than ever. Until her mom was home again, if Cassidy had to be in the house at all, she was going to bring somebody with her.

She drove to school, wondering what she would tell Dr. Randall. Or more to the point, what Dr. Randall would make her tell.

* * *

"There's something funny going on." Matt hadn't touched a bite of the food on his plate. Cafeteria lunches were pretty awful, but the enchiladas weren't bad. He usually liked those.

"What do you mean, funny?" asked Cassidy. She forked another bite into her mouth. She normally didn't eat here, but the smell of the enchiladas had persuaded her.

"How would anyone know we had anything to steal, I mean, any documents about Annie?"

Cassidy noticed that even Matt had stopped calling Annie her mother. It was easier to distinguish them this way. Cassidy's parent, her mother, was Mary Thornton. Annie Logan was someone from another life.

"You didn't tell anyone, did you?" he asked.

"Only you two."

"You didn't tell the shrink?" asked Rory.

She thought about it, then said, "No, I haven't mentioned any of this to him. I only told him about the memories coming back. That was enough to make him think I'm going nuts. No, I'm sure I didn't tell him anything about searching for her records. I was too scared. He really would have thought I was crazy, then."

"What's with this guy?" said Matt. "I thought he was supposed to be helping you, not making you feel worse about yourself. What kind of psychiatrist is he?"

"A friend of the family," said Cassidy. "At least, that's what my dad tells me."

"Some friend," said Rory.

"Okay, let's not get distracted," said Matt. "If the shrink didn't know about the records, who did?"

Cassidy thought, but couldn't think of anyone.

"I didn't even tell my mom," said Rory, "so don't look at me."

"Well I sure didn't say anything," said Matt.

"Not even to your dad?" Rory asked.

"Nope, not even to him. I don't think he would have been too thrilled with the way we came by some of the information."

"I thought you said it was legal," said Rory.

"It was . . . sort of."

"Oh great," Rory complained, "so now we're breaking the law, too."

"I didn't say we were breaking the law. We just bent it a little. And you're getting us off the track again. Who would know about the documents?"

"I guess a cop could find out," said Cassidy.

"A cop? You mean Terrell?" asked Matt.

She nodded. "I guess he could, if he wanted to know what we've been doing. Cops have access to a bunch of records. Maybe someone told him we've been snooping."

"Come on," said Rory, "that's too weird."

"I don't know," said Matt. "I think maybe she's right about this. Terrell might be the only one who could know—him, or another cop."

Cassidy lost her appetite. She had hoped Matt would say her idea was wrong, but he thought it was a possibility. That conclusion ruined any hope of finishing lunch. Her stomach clenched into a tight, hard ball. There was no way she could even swallow, much less enjoy eating.

"I'm going to see what I can find out about Officer John Terrell," said Matt. "I think we'd better take a harder look at this guy, and see what's going on. If he was connected with Annie, I think it's time we find out about it."

Rory glanced at Cassidy. Neither one said anything. The wheels were turning. Events were in motion, and there didn't seem to be any way for Cassidy to stop them. The truth was, she wouldn't stop them even if she could. Maybe she'd found out too much. Or maybe she was too curious for her own good. Either way, it had gone too far.

At first, all she'd wanted was to know about her birth mother. Now, she wanted everything. She wanted to know who killed Annie, and why. Beyond this, she wanted to unlock all the memories that were hidden in her mind.

Annie Logan's death had happened to Cassidy, too. She had lost a mother. She had almost lost her mind. Whoever killed Annie had a debt to pay, not only for what he'd done to Annie, but for what he'd done to Cassidy, too. *And my parents,* she added, thinking of the stress that had put her mother in the hospital with a heart condition.

Someone was guilty. Cassidy was going to find him.

If her father hadn't insisted, she wouldn't have ever seen Dr. Randall again. Simply driving to his office filled her with so much nervousness that her heart was pounding and her hands were shaking by the time she reached the parking lot. He scared her; there was no other term for this feeling.

The building seemed as cold as Randall himself, mirrored steel and glass. She didn't look at her reflection as she passed through the entrance. Didn't want to see the fear in her eyes.

She stepped into the elevator and pressed the button for the seventh floor. Dr. Randall's suite of offices occupied the entire seventh floor. His name was etched in gold on the interior double doors as she stepped off the elevator.

Don't go. The warning shivered in her mind, rippling across her thoughts. *Turn around now; it's not too late.*

"Cassidy," called out Sharon the receptionist, who happened to be walking along the hall behind Cassidy, heading toward the office, "Dr. Randall has been anxious to see you. Come right in." She held open the glass door.

Whatever moment there had been to turn back was now lost. She was feeling sick with fear, nauseated, cold, perspiring. Not sure she could stand, Cassidy took the seat nearest the window, trying to calm herself by looking out. There were ordinary people out there, with ordinary lives. She saw a young mother and her child walking along the sidewalk, a boy on his bicycle, and passing cars full of strangers who were driving to places that didn't terrify them.

Like this place terrified her.

"Come in, Cassidy," said Dr. Randall. She hadn't seen him approach her. He was standing right beside her chair. With what seemed like a kind gesture, he reached over and took her hand.

His touch made her gasp. She drew her hand out of his hold. His eyes narrowed at this obvious snub. He stood back, the palms of both hands turned up, as if showing he was quite innocent. "You're jumpy today. We'll talk about that."

Cassidy tried not to let him see how nervous she was, being here. She crossed her arms when she moved past him, so he wouldn't see the trembling of her hands. A hard pulse was beating a tattoo at her temples, and a droning like loud static was humming in her ears.

Going into Randall's office and hearing him close the door after her was like stepping into an interrogation chamber, where prisoners were tortured. That's how she felt, as if she were about to be tortured, and couldn't reveal the secrets.

Thirteen

"Sit down, please. You don't look well, Cassidy."

She sat in the leather chair opposite his desk. She thought of the living animal that had worn the skin on this chair, and the thought revolted her. A man like Dr. Randall would have leather upholstered furniture. It was like him.

"Your father's concerned about you," he began. "I must admit, seeing you look as you do, I'm concerned, too. Have the nightmares become worse lately? Is that what's happening, Cassidy?"

She didn't want to look at his face, into the intimidating track of his eyes. She glanced down at her clasped hands, at the carpet, at her shoes. Anywhere, but at him.

"I think I'm all right. I've been worried about my mother. That's normal, isn't it?"

"About your mother in the hospital?"

This specifying of mothers surprised her. "Yes, of course her. Who else?"

"I thought you might have meant your birth mother. You've been giving her a lot of thought, too, haven't you? Please don't deny it. I can read the evidence of these thoughts in your eyes. It's your concern over the circumstances of your birth mother's death that has caused you all this anxiety. That's true, isn't it?"

She didn't answer.

He waited. When it was clear she wouldn't respond, he asked, "What have you done about investigating her murder? You've been trying to piece it together, and in doing so, you're tearing yourself apart."

How could he know this? He acted as if he were sure about things she'd never told him.

"I've been curious about her, about what happened, but I haven't—"

"Don't lie to me!"

His sudden anger shocked her. She did glance up, and his eyes were no longer simply intimidating, but vivid threats. He was glaring, and there was an ugliness to his face that she hadn't seen before. His features, which had seemed so sophisticated, now looked crude and coarse. His eyebrows were beetled into hairy slugs over the dark menace of his eyes.

She pushed back her chair, ready to stand and rush from the room.

"Sit there until I tell you to leave." He came around the desk and stood beside her chair, looming over her. "I've had enough of your games of silence, Cassidy. You'll talk to me this morning, or you will not leave this office."

"You can't keep me here."

"No, you're right about that." He finger-stabbed the button on his intercom. "Sharon, I'd like you to arrange a room for Cassidy Thornton in the locked ward of Braitwithe Sanitarium. It will be for an observation period of not less than seventy-two hours."

"Yes, doctor."

"I want to talk to my father," Cassidy cried.

"I'm sorry, that isn't possible right now."

He turned from the intercom and placed his hands on Cassidy's chair. "Now, we can do it either way. It's your choice, you see. I would prefer you to tell me about what you've been up to—we'll handle it right here—but if you force me, Cassidy, I will follow this through with whatever measures it takes. You shouldn't doubt that."

She didn't. She believed Dr. Randall would have her locked in a mental hospital faster than anyone could stop him, or find her. "What do you want to know?"

"That's better," he said, taking his seat behind the desk again. "That's cooperative. Tell me, have you been searching into your mother's legal documents?"

"Yes."

He didn't ask for specifics, which surprised her, but went on with this line of questioning. "I assume you've found your birth certificate and other court records?"

"Yes."

"And you've read the account of her murder in the papers?"

"No."

"Really? I'm disappointed. I assumed you had.

You've been so clever. Let me get it for you. You'll read it now. I'd like to have your reaction."

He went to a locked file drawer in the corner of the room, drew out the key from a cluster of those in his pocket, and opened the lower drawer. It took some rummaging around, but he came up with the newspaper clipping and brought it to her.

The paper was yellowed with age, and brown along the borders. A large black-and-white photo was framed at the center of the page. It was a picture of a woman's body sprawled on a grassy slope. There were dark stains along the paler tones of her throat and clothing. The darker stains were blood.

The headline read: Two-Year-Old Found On The Body Of Her Dead Mother. Below the photo was the caption: Brutal death witnessed by victim's child.

Cassidy stared at the printed page, stared at the photo of Annie Logan, and tried to find sense in the image, or some awareness of what had happened that day so long ago, but she couldn't remember.

"Read the newspaper account, Cassidy," said Dr. Randall. "I think it will help you. After all, you've come this far. You want to know all of it, don't you? Read."

"Could I take it home with me?"

He smiled. "Read it here."

"Please, I want to go home."

"I'm not sure that's going to happen, at least

not today. You're being . . . difficult. Will you read the paper, Cassidy? Or shall I put it away?"

And put me away, too, she thought. She began reading.

> *The body of local resident, Anne Logan, was found in Arroyo Seco Park by a jogger this morning. The victim had been repeatedly stabbed sometime during the night. The most horrifying aspect of this murder was that a child of approximately two years of age was found sitting atop the dead woman's body.*

Cassidy felt a flood of emotion and memory course through her at reading these words. She had been that child. Anne Logan, Annie, had been her mother.

"Horrifying, isn't it?" said Dr. Randall. "It was a shock to everyone, the entire community was buzzing over it for weeks. Of course, eventually talk dies down and people go on with their lives. They forget the details of the incident and find something new to interest them. But you didn't, did you?"

"I was part of it. Annie was my mother. I saw it happen."

"You did, yes. That was unfortunate. I'm sure the man who killed your mother didn't intend you to be a witness. Such things are usually done without witnesses. But then, you were so young. I suppose he thought you wouldn't remember. What do you remember, Cassidy?"

She didn't like the way he asked the question.

Now she was angry, not just scared, but angry at the way she was being treated. She wanted to shock him. "I remember everything. I know what happened that night, and I know who did it."

Randall stepped back, as if calculating the situation. "Do you?"

Now, she wished she hadn't said it.

"How long have you known?"

She decided to bluff her way through. "This week. I finally realized who I'd been seeing, and then it all made sense." She thought of her flashbacks of Annie arguing in the yard with John Terrell.

"You're amazing," said Dr. Randall. "Most people can't remember anything from when they were two. Of course, it was a traumatic event, something that stayed longer in your memory. And the nightmares have restored a lot of it for you, haven't they?"

She took a risk. "It's like Annie wants me to know the truth."

That hit a nerve. "The truth! You think that's what you've seen with your nightmares and flashbacks? Do you believe for even one moment that anything you've imagined would be allowed as testimony in a court of law?"

"I didn't say—"

"Your testimony would be thrown out of court as wild supposition and a too vivid imagination, or insanity. You have a history of mental disorder, don't forget. Any lawyer would be sure to bring up that point."

"I wasn't talking about going to court. I was talking about knowing my mother's killer."

That stopped his ranting. His voice changed to a soft-spoken, almost pleading, quality. "Yes, that's what you said. How is it you believe you do know him, may I ask?"

"Because I remember hearing Annie call his name, right before he killed her."

"Tell me what you remember."

It was all so real now. Cassidy felt the terror of that night surround and overwhelm her. "I was sitting in the swing. There was a squirrel on the grass. I was watching it. And then I heard a noise, the sound of someone walking through the trees and over the scattered leaves on the grass. Annie heard it, too. She told him, 'Go away.' And then she turned around and . . ."

Cassidy glanced up. The expression on Dr. Randall's face shocked her. He looked grief stricken, and there were tears brimming in his eyes.

"You do remember it," he whispered.

He was scaring her. He was supposed to be a psychiatrist, and he was scaring her into a panic. What kind of professional medical behavior was this, crying and shouting at her? She'd had enough.

"I'm leaving. I'm going home right now."

Sharon, the receptionist, knocked and entered the room. "Excuse me, doctor, but the orderlies from Braitwithe are here."

Behind Sharon, Cassidy could see two burly-looking men in white suits, the uniform of orderlies.

"No!" cried Cassidy, standing and backing against the window. Below her, people walked along the sidewalk as if everything were normal. Here, on the seventh floor, normal had turned to crazy, and she was caught in the trap of it.

"You'll only make it worse for yourself if you struggle," said Dr. Randall.

The two men were moving toward her. Dr. Randall had a syringe in his hand. *Where had that come from? Did he have it all along?*

"Leave me alone! I'm not crazy!" she screamed.

"It's all right," said the bigger of the two orderlies. "We aren't going to hurt you. Take it easy. You're safe."

She lunged beneath his outstretched arms and raced for the door.

"Grab her, Mike!" he said. "Don't let her get away!"

Cassidy tore past Mike, and Dr. Randall. She felt her heartbeat in her throat, pounding fear into her brain. *Run.* She made it to the waiting room, past Sharon with the startled look in her eyes, and out through the glass doors.

They were right behind. The floor vibrated with the heavy thuds of their steps racing for her. She could hear the hard grunt of someone's breath as he ran.

"Help me!" she screamed. "Somebody help me!"

There was only one woman in the hallway. She turned and stared at Cassidy, then clutched her purse to her ample bosom.

The elevator door opened. The woman must

have pushed the button. Cassidy almost ran to it, but she knew there wasn't time. Randall and the two men were at her heels. If she stepped into the elevator, they would grab her. She headed for the stairs.

The stairwell door was heavy. It pulled the muscles of her arm as she yanked it back. She gave one quick glance to see if the door could be locked behind her, but there was nothing on the inside panel. It was a standard fire exit.

She took the steps three at a time, jumping to the landing. The door opened above her and she heard them on the stairs. Cassidy had one advantage: she was younger and weighed less. She could move faster. She held onto the rail and jumped the next three steps.

Her foot landed badly. The right ankle twisted beneath her. There was a sharp popping sound, like something coming out of place. Everything in her world was out of place, and now she couldn't run.

Trying to move on that ankle felt like forcing a steel rod through her leg. Her knee buckled. The right leg caved and she fell. They were just above her, two of them, Randall and one of the orderlies.

Where was the other one?

Below her, on the next level, the door opened. The second orderly stepped onto the fifth floor landing and started up the steps. Randall and the first orderly headed down the stairs.

She was trapped between them.

Cassidy grabbed the railing and pulled herself

to her feet. Pain shot white-hot agony through her injured foot and leg. She leaned over the stairwell, a sheer drop of five stories. Jumping was the only way to escape them. The distance looked deceptively close. Maybe she could survive it.

"Don't do anything foolish," said the orderly approaching her from below. "We're here to help you."

"She's suicidal," said Dr. Randall. He held back while the first orderly slowed his pace, but steadily came down the stairs toward her.

I'm not suicidal, thought Cassidy. She would never think of killing herself, not even now. The fall was too far. She moved back from the railing, sat on the step, huddled with her arms wrapped over her knees, and waited for the two hospital attendants to grab her.

The crush of an arm pinned her.

"It's okay, we've got her."

She saw Dr. Randall's eyes, and felt the prick of a needle as whatever drug was in the syringe entered her body. All the fight left her, and as if she had leaned too far over the railing, she felt herself falling into a deadly and bottomless dark.

Fourteen

It was hard to distinguish the fine line between her dream, and reality. Was she awake, or was this room part of the nightmare of being chased?

Where am I?

She tried to rise from the bed, but her head felt so dizzy she couldn't sit. There were guardrails on the bed! This was crazy. *Crazy.*

Everything returned, the memory of racing out of Dr. Randall's office, of the two men from the mental hospital, and of being trapped in the stairwell. They'd given her some drug, the shot Dr. Randall forced into her arm.

Panic struck in the quick beats of her heart against her ribs. *What am I going to do? How do I get out of here?*

She looked around. The room was small, not much bigger than the space of the bed, sided by the width of one chair, and a little walking around area. There were drawn curtains on the far wall, and a door that looked as if it might lead to a hospital-sized bathroom. Plus the door out.

Cassidy focused on that. She didn't see a phone in her room, or any way to contact her dad, or a friend. The only way out of this place was through that door. She could open it quietly, sneak past the nursing station—if there was one—and beat it out of here before anyone noticed she was gone. The trick was getting out of bed.

She tried sitting again. When she lifted her head beyond the height of an inch or two off the pillow, the room tilted and started rolling around. She grabbed the rail and hung on, pulling herself to a sitting position by sheer will. Now, the room did circles above, before, and below her.

I'm going to puke, she thought, miserably. But maybe puking was okay. It might help get whatever drug Randall had given her out of her system. Very carefully, trying not to fall over the edge, she climbed the guardrail and set one foot on the floor. Her leg shook as she tested her weight on it. She was careful not to let go of the guardrail until both feet were flat on the cold linoleum.

Try to focus on one thing, she thought, fighting the wave of nausea and dizziness. She stared at the floor, trying to steady herself until the room came into one unwavering image. That took some doing. At first, she saw four feet, then three. By the time she saw only two and a half, she'd also noticed something else. She was dressed in a hospital gown.

Her impulse was to climb back in bed, pull up the covers, and pack it in until the nightmare went away. But this was no nightmare. This was real, and if she didn't get out of here right now—hospital gown, or not—she might be stuck in this place for a very long time.

There wasn't any choice.

One foot in front of the other. The first step was the hard one. Almost fell there. Steady. Okay, two more steps. Not so bad. Stumbled a little, but didn't drop. Only a couple more steps to the door. One. Two. Made it!

She grabbed for the handle. Only, there wasn't one. *Come on, come on,* she thought, believing she'd missed it somehow. Maybe it fell into that vortex at the bottom of the spinning room. Palms pressed flat to the smooth metal, she slid them over the surface of the door. Nothing. No doorknob, no latch, no handle.

A locked ward. That was what Dr. Randall had threatened.

Frustration raged within her. She wanted to pound her fists on the door and scream—Let me out of here! But she didn't, because then they'd know she was up and out of bed.

Tears of self-pity misted in her eyes. She blinked them back. Anger was a stronger emotion. It gave her the courage to act. If the door was locked, then it would have to be the window.

The trip across the length of the room was exhausting. Staggering, she tripped once and saved herself from a fall by grabbing the chair. It wasn't the fall she feared, but the noise. At last, the window was before her. She pushed back the heavy curtains and looked out. Her room was three stories off the ground.

I don't care, she thought. Nothing mattered anymore, except getting out of here. There was a metal awning one floor down—it would break her fall—and a fire escape below that.

Break the window and get out. Hurry, before someone comes.

The thought that it was a crazy thing to do hit her, just as she picked up the chair and struck it against the window. Maybe she wouldn't jump, but she could scream for help.

Except the window didn't break.

She swung the chair again, realizing she was weak, but knowing, too, that she was putting all her strength into the action. The chair hit, and bounced off the glass. Nothing happened, except it made a lot of racket.

She heard a jingle of keys at the lock. The door swung open. A middle-aged woman in a white nurse's uniform stood in the doorway. "Put that chair down, now!"

Cassidy froze, still holding the chair raised above her head. The woman looked angry enough to strike her.

"I need assistance in here!" the woman yelled down the hall. "A combative patient in 3-A."

The sound of running footsteps alerted Cassidy that others were coming. "Please," she tried to explain, "you don't understand. I'm not supposed to be here. My father . . . let me call my father."

The nurse advanced on her. "Put that chair down. Do it now!"

The two orderlies who'd trapped Cassidy in the

stairwell of Dr. Randall's office appeared in the doorway. "Randall said she's suicidal," one of them said to the nurse.

"I'm not. He's lying." Cassidy felt the swirling motion of the room grow worse with every moment of her heightened panic. "I would never take my life."

"You were trying to break that window and jump," said the nurse.

Was I? thought Cassidy. Suddenly, she was confused and afraid. She had thought of jumping . . . but not to her death. She only wanted to get away. It wasn't like they said. She'd never thought of killing herself.

The nurse advanced again, and Cassidy swung the chair in her direction. "Stay back! Leave me alone."

"We don't allow such behavior here," said the nurse. Cassidy could see her eyes; they were green and luminous as a watch dial.

"Be careful, Rose," said one of the men. "She ought to be knocked out cold, with what the doc gave her, but this one's a fighter."

"I'm always careful," said Rose, "and I'll thank you to save your comments on medication for the employees' lounge. It's not for the patients to overhear."

The three of them came at Cassidy. She tried to fend them off with the chair, holding it in front of her like a lion tamer, but one of the men grabbed a chair leg and yanked it out of her hands. Then they had her.

One of them pinned her to the ground, while another wrestled with her, forcing her arms into the sleeves of a white jacket. The sleeves were sewn shut at the ends. She was so dizzy, and so sick. All her energy to fight was gone. Two of them hauled her to a sitting position, pinning her jacketed arms across her chest, while the woman buckled the straps at the ends of the jacket's sleeves to fasteners at the back.

"That ought to keep her out of trouble," said one of the orderlies.

Cassidy tried to move her arms, but they were crisscrossed and held in place by the buckles at the back of the straitjacket. She struggled, but it was useless. "Why are you doing this to me?" she cried.

"We're trying to help you," said the nurse. "Get back into your bed and lie down," she ordered. "Do it at once, or we'll have to use restraints to hold you onto the bed."

Cassidy didn't want any more restraints. She rolled to her side, pushed her body up to her knees, and stood without any of them offering her any assistance. The nurse's eyes were still glaring anger. *I've made an enemy*, thought Cassidy, *and just when I needed a friend*.

She climbed onto the bed and lay down, exactly as Rose the nurse had told her.

"That's better," said Rose. "Take that chair out of here," Rose told one of the orderlies. "She won't be needing it anymore."

Cassidy was afraid to say anything, or move. Everything she'd done had been interpreted as violent. She needed to win the trust of Rose, the orderlies, or someone in this hospital—if she was ever going to get out of here.

"I'll have to tell Dr. Randall about this incident," the nurse said to Cassidy. "He may want to change your medication to something stronger, for your protection."

Something stronger! Anything stronger and Cassidy would be a vegetable. She couldn't see straight now. Did he mean to keep her unconscious?

"You behave yourself," said Rose, then she and the orderlies left the room.

Cassidy heard the tumblers of the lock turn in the door. Now she was alone, staitjacketed, drugged, and locked in a mental ward . . .

Dr. Randall came to see Cassidy after dinnertime that evening. He was in a different suit, looking much calmer than he had that afternoon. His attention seemed to be on the chart, for he didn't glance at her.

"The ward nurse says you caused some trouble for them. That won't be tolerated here, Cassidy. This isn't home and you can't bully the staff. I'm sorry about the straitjacket, but I do understand why they felt it was necessary. This is a locked mental ward. Any behavior such as you demonstrated will be viewed as violent, and dealt with accordingly."

He did glance at her. Once.

"I've left approval for a syringe of a medication

to control all such outbursts, if it should become necessary. They have my permission to use it at their discretion. It's entirely up to you."

She glared at him. "Why are you doing this to me?"

He shook his head, a sad expression on his face. "I'm not doing anything to you, Cassidy. I'm trying to save your life. You forget, I've seen how your emotional state deteriorated before. You're older, and more capable of harming yourself. I can't stand by and let that happen. I had to take appropriate action . . . for your own good."

She wanted to scream. Instead, she forced her voice to remain calm. "Tell them to take this jacket off."

"I'm not sure they'd think that was a good idea," he said.

"You're the doctor. They have to listen to you. Tell them to do it, and they will."

Surprisingly, he seemed to be considering this option. "If I made a bargain with you, if I do as you say, would I have your word not to try anything stupid?"

"Yes."

He backed away and stared into her eyes, as if reading them. "You won't try to hurt yourself, throw yourself down a stairwell, or out of the window of a building? Do you promise me?"

"Yes, I promise."

He rubbed his brow with his long, narrow fingers. "All right," he said at last. "I'm going to trust you." With maddening slowness, Dr. Randall released the straps.

Cassidy rubbed her arms. They ached from confinement in the restraints. She couldn't do more than stretch her arms; the jacket was still fastened at the back.

"This was never what I wanted," Randall told her as he released the buckles one by one. "I like to use kindness with my patients. It's always best, but when they resist treatment as you did . . ." He pulled the jacket open at the back, and came around in front of her. "There," he said, tugging on the sleeves and pulling the straitjacket off.

She made no sudden moves. *If I cooperate*, she thought, *he'll let me out of here.* "I want to see my father. Will you call him, please?" She said it sweetly, like a child in first grade to her teacher.

"That isn't possible. I'm afraid I'll have to refuse permission for you to see or speak to your parents for a while. They would be too sympathetic, and that's part of the problem, as I see it. You know how to work their sympathies, don't you, Cassidy? No, I've spoken to your father and explained to him that for this period of observation, it would be better if there were no visits from your family."

"I just want to talk to him."

His lips didn't smile, but his eyes seemed to. "I can't allow it. Your father's in perfect agreement with me on this."

"That isn't true! My father wouldn't do this to me. Never. What did you tell him? What lie? My father would never leave me in a place like this, not if he knew. I don't believe you."

"Would you feel better if you saw his signature on the form? I want you to be completely at ease about being here. Really, he thought it would be best, especially since your mother is so ill."

"Liar!"

"You've caused your parents a great deal of strain, Cassidy. Your mother's heart condition, and your father's ulcer. Did he tell you he has a very serious ulcer? It's something you should know."

She wanted to scratch Dr. Randall's face, to dig her nails into the smug wall of his face and drag them down till the claw marks flowed bright red. She'd never hated anyone before, but she hated Dr. Randall.

"I have to be going now," he said, and headed for the door. She ran, but he was faster. The door locked from the outside.

"The nurse will be by later with your evening medication. I advise you to take it, if you don't want the straitjacket again. I'll see you tomorrow, and we'll talk about your sleep, and your dreams."

Her dreams had put her in this place, Dr. Randall's obsessive interest in her dreams. What was he trying to find out? And when he knew the answer, would he let her go?

The questions silvered like fire over her brain, touched a nerve, and stayed. All night, the question repeated: *Will he ever let me go?*

Fifteen

Morning was being forced awake at dawn, when she had just fallen asleep a couple of hours before. Sleep had seemed impossible, but sometime before morning, her eyes had finally closed. Now, she was desperate with the need for rest, but the ward nurse insisted Cassidy come to the dining room with the other patients and have "a hearty breakfast."

She felt more like throwing up than eating breakfast, but no one asked her. The staff didn't seem to care how she felt, they simply told her what to do. She followed, walking on steadier legs than yesterday, but exhausted.

The dining room was a long, dormitory-type hall, with a row of tables lined end to end, and benches bordering the sides. Cassidy looked at the other guests of Braitwithe Sanitarium. Some were young, like her. Others were closer to her mother's age.

There were two at the end of the table who might have been any age; it was impossible to tell. One's face was badly deformed, with a misshapen, nearly flat nose, and a hole in her top lip that gaped open to the roof of her mouth. The other one, a man, had been burned sometime during his life. Cassidy couldn't estimate his age from the tracks of reddened scar tissue that was left of his face. His hair had been burned, too. He had tufts of brown hair that grew along one side of his scalp and in skimpy patches around the back of his head.

"Come and sit here," said the dining hall attendant. She pulled out a chair for Cassidy. It was right across from the two at the end of the table. "We're a little crowded this morning," the attendant said, "but we've made room for you—next to Robin and Bill."

Cassidy sat, and a dark-haired man put a plate before her. Egg whites glistened up at her from the food. It was meant to be scrambled eggs, she could tell from the clumped shape, but the yellow and the whites hadn't been blended. The whites were runny looking, wet, and slimy. The toast was slathered with butter, too, greasy and thick. The bacon was fatty and undercooked. "I don't want this," she said, moving the nauseating mess away.

"Are you going to give us trouble this morning?" said the room attendant. She squeezed Cassidy's arm till it hurt.

"Ow. I just don't want any breakfast."

"Oh, you don't?" There was a menacing glint in the woman's eyes.

Cassidy realized she'd made a big mistake.

"It's not good enough for you? Is that what's wrong?"

"No—it looks great. I feel a little sick today, from the medication, that's all." She tried to look sincere. "I like scrambled eggs."

"I don't like to see good food wasted," said the attendant.

"No, 'course not." Cassidy forked a bite of the eggs into her mouth. It had the consistency and taste of thick mayonnaise on her tongue.

The attendant stayed where she was and watched until Cassidy swallowed. "You'll feel stronger when you get some nourishment into you." The woman's attention was distracted by a small disturbance at the other end of the table. "Tom, what are you doing? Stop playing with your food." She moved away.

"If you don't want your breakfast," whispered Bill, "I'll eat it for you. Slide it onto my plate when the watchdog's not looking."

Cassidy glanced conspiratorially down the length of the table, where the straight back of the attendant stood guard at the side of the offending diners. If she got caught, she knew there would be hell to pay, but looking at the globs of fat bubbled on the surface of the food, she figured it was worth the risk. In one deft motion, she switched plates with Bill.

He started eating immediately, shoveling eggs and bacon into his mouth in three or four huge bites. He was finishing the last of the toast by the time the attendant looked back in their direction.

"Thank you," whispered Cassidy.

"Next time, if there's stuff you don't want," he

said, "we'll share it with Robin, too. They don't give her very much."

Cassidy glanced at Robin. She was thin.

"Robin's okay in the head," said Bill. "She's here because of her cleft palate. Her folks didn't want her. She can't talk too good, but she's smart."

"That's terrible." It shocked her that anyone would put a person in a place like this because of a physical deformity. "How long has she been here?"

"Five years," said Bill, swallowing the last bite of toast.

Five years! It wasn't possible. Surely some inspector from the state must have come to this sanitarium during that length of time and seen that she was normal, except for her handicap. The idea that they hadn't done so left Cassidy feeling cold and shaky.

If no one checked the system . . . how long would Cassidy be trapped here?

She didn't want to be rude, but she had to ask. "And you're here because . . ."

"Isn't it obvious?" asked Bill. "Nobody in my family wanted to look at me, after the fire. That was a long time ago. I don't count the years anymore. What does it get you? They said I was crazy, suicidal, and paid one of the doctors to have me committed."

Cassidy was horrified. "Can they do that?"

Bill's eyes met hers for the first time. "You're asking me? You ought to know the answer. Everyone's heard about you."

It wasn't the same. Her family hadn't put her here to get rid of her. They'd never do that. Still, her father's signature had been on the admissions sheet. He'd signed the form. It was hard to get that image out of her mind. Why would her dad have agreed to put her in this place, and not even come to see her? Tears burned at the corners of Cassidy's eyes.

"Don't feel bad," said Bill. "The doctors get a bundle for keeping us here."

"I don't believe you," she cried. Tears ran down her cheeks.

Robin's hand touched hers. "Issh she all right. Don' cry, Casshhidy."

She hadn't realized Robin could speak.

"Issh not ssho bad. We'll help 'ou."

Help her? How?

The day was only an hour old, and it was already awful. Cassidy felt like screaming, throwing a tantrum, beating her fists on the table and screaming. But that would lead to the straitjacket, and the orderlies, and the drugs. She held her rage inside her, and waited. She had an advantage over most of Braitwithe's guests. Like Bill and Robin, Cassidy wasn't crazy. She'd follow the rules and do everything they told her.

Sooner or later, her chance would come . . . and then she'd find a way out of here.

Midmorning, Cassidy was allowed to mingle with a few other patients in the recreation room. The area was wide and sunny, with windows made of the same unbreakable material Cassidy had in her locked room. This area was attractive, colorful with potted plants, bright-patterned sofas and chairs, and tables full of games and recreational equipment.

It was the only area of the sanitarium where visitors were allowed, Cassidy found out. Bill told her.

Bill didn't mind the sanitarium so much. He missed his freedom, he said, and most people here were a little off-center, but at least nobody made fun of him. "People can be cruel to somebody who looks like me," he said, "and not just kids."

Cassidy imagined that was true. She remembered how she'd felt the first time she saw Bill. If she'd been on the street, she probably would have turned away and not spoken to him.

For Bill, the sanitarium was safe, up to a point. "Sometimes, you see things that go on in here that turn your stomach."

"What do you mean?" Cassidy felt a cold shiver inside her.

"Years ago, there was this woman . . . Rebecca Finley. There was nothin' wrong with her. She wasn't like them," he waved his hand in the direction of the other patients. "I could tell."

"Why was she here, then?"

"Dr. Randall said she was crazy, suicidal. Said she had to be locked up for her own protection. There wasn't nothing wrong with Rebecca that getting a divorce from her husband wouldn't have fixed. He was the real reason she was in this place, and why she never left—leastwise, not alive."

"She died?"

Bill nodded. "There was a big fuss made after they found her overdosed, nurses and orderlies getting blamed for leaving narcotics around where patients could get hold of them. That was nothing new. Half the orderlies in this sanitarium pinch a little of the patients' drugs. It's like a side benefit to working here."

Cassidy had to be clear on what she'd heard. "She died here, in Braitwithe?"

"Um-hmm."

"And Randall was her doctor?"

"Oh yeah, but he was just getting started back then. I remember seeing the bottom of his shoes when he came here, and one of them had a big hole in it. He wasn't rich, like he is now."

Cassidy was trying to understand, trying to put the pieces of the puzzle together. "You think he deliberately kept that woman here, and . . ."

"Overdosed her," said Bill. "That's what he did. Called it a suicide."

"But, why?"

Bill glanced around, then nervously rubbed his neck with his wide, meaty hand. Christy hadn't noticed until then how big Bill's hands were, like small shovels. His arms were beefy, too. They looked strong enough to lift weights.

"All I know is, after Rebecca Finley died, Dr. Randall had new shoes, a new suit, fine clothes. He didn't work around-the-clock shifts like he had before, either. He came in now and again, saw a few patients, but his life had changed."

"How?"

"That woman was rich—had been, anyway—and when she died, her husband and Dr. Randall split the estate. That's what I heard."

Cassidy's throat tightened. She was having trouble taking the next breath. "He killed her? Dr. Randall killed his patient?"

"Now you've got it," said Bill. "He overdosed her, made her death look like a suicide, but he killed her for the money."

A nurse came into the recreation room. "All right, everyone. Time for morning medications. Leave what you're doing now and go back to your rooms."

Bill started for the door.

"Wait," Cassidy called after him. "I want to know—"

Bill shot her a glance that left no doubt as to its meaning. Without uttering a word, his message was loud and clear: *Not now, the nurse will hear you.*

Cassidy figured it out, but too late. The nurse had noticed. She crossed the room to Cassidy. "Was there something you wanted from Bill?" Suspicion showed in her eyes.

If Cassidy said no, it would seem like a lie. She had to think of something to tell the woman, anything to satisfy her piqued curiosity. "I wanted to ask how he was burned."

The nurse's distrustful expression softened into plain dislike. "That's none of your business. Bill doesn't want to talk about his appearance. It's rude to ask such personal questions. Now, go back to your room and stop being such a little busybody."

Cassidy walked away at once. She didn't take her next breath until the nurse was ten feet behind her. That had been a close one. Had to be more careful. Showing too much interest in fellow patients could be dangerous in this place. How many other secrets did Braitwithe hide behind locked doors?

Was the staff part of the schemes? Did they know what Dr. Randall had done, and was doing? Cassidy couldn't take any chances. If she talked to the wrong person, it could mean her death.

She walked along the corridor which led to the wards. It was empty, except for one patient heading toward her. He was dressed in a blue sweat suit, not gray like the ones from this wing of the sanitarium. Some other kind of patient.

Cassidy was thinking about the suspicious nurse, Dr. Randall, the story of the murdered woman, and how she was going to get out of here. She wasn't paying much attention to the other patient—not until they were almost face-to-face in the hallway.

"Cassidy? Is that really you?"

She looked up. Standing right next to her was Brian Perry, her friend, the driver from the car accident.

Sixteen

Cassidy couldn't believe it—Brian here. She didn't stop to figure out why. Whatever the reason, she was going to make use of this opportunity. She glanced around, but didn't see any lurking floor attendants or nurses. Without explanation, she grabbed Brian's hand and pulled him into a recessed doorway.

"Can you get a call out?"

"What?" asked Brian, obviously surprised and confused by the question. "I can't believe I'm seeing you here, Cassi. This place is—"

"Brian, this is important. They won't let me leave, Or make a call. I need help to get out of here. Can you call someone for me?" She glanced down the hall. "Quickly, before someone comes."

"Yeah, sure. I can call anybody I want. I'm here voluntarily, the alcohol abuse program. My parents insisted, after I plowed the car into that retaining wall." His expression said he had finally noticed the difference in the color of their Braitwithe sweat suits. "What kind of ward is this, Cassi?"

She didn't have the energy to think of a lie. "It's the loony bin. Now, listen to me. There isn't much time. I need help. Will you call someone for me? Tell him I'm here against my will?"

She could imagine what Brian must be thinking: *locked in the mental ward, telling everybody she's here against her will.* He probably figured she was crazy. Probably believed she—

"Tell me who to call," he said. "I'll do it right now."

"Oh, Brian." She was overwhelmed with relief.

"Hey, you were there for me once. Maybe I can help you now."

She heard the noise of a door opening at the far end of the corridor. They had to hurry. She wanted to tell him to call her father and mother, but if what Dr. Randall had told her was true, they already knew she was here. Instead, she told Brian the name of first person she thought of. "Do you know Rory Spencer?"

He looked blank. "No."

"How about Matt Austin?"

There were footsteps coming up the corridor.

"Yeah sure, I know Matt."

Thank God! "Call him. Tell him Dr. Randall is a killer."

"Say what?"

"Tell Matt I need his help. Will you do that for me, Bri?"

Whoever was walking toward them was almost there. Cassidy felt terror building in her like a raging fire. "I'm not suicidal. Tell him that. And ask him to look up the files of a Rebecca Finley, one of Dr. Randall's former patients."

There wasn't any more time. Another step or two, and the person in the hall would see them. Brian moved fast, rushing out of the doorway alcove and bumping right into the ward nurse. Cassidy recognized the voice when the woman complained about being jostled.

"Watch where you're going! What's the matter with you, anyway?" the nurse demanded, irritation dripping like acid from her voice. "And what are you doing in this corridor? You're part of the alcohol abuse program. You don't belong in this wing."

"Boy, am I glad to see you," said Brian. "I'm all turned around in this place. I was looking for the rec room. I was told I could pick up a couple of pieces of equipment there, Ping-Pong paddles and some games. I can't find the place anywhere."

"Who sent you here?" asked the nurse, still sounding irritated, but less suspicious.

"That dude in the green hat—what's his name—"

"David Morse."

"Yeah, Dave. He told me I might find the stuff here."

Cassidy's heart was beating at twice its normal speed. *Go with him to the rec room,* she thought. *Go with him.*

"You can't be wandering around unaccompanied on this ward."

"The door was open."

"Yes, it's always unlocked, but our mental patients use this area for recreation from nine-thirty to eleven. You might have run into one of them. It isn't safe for you."

"Mental patients, huh. Hey, lady, I don't want to run into any crazies. A bunch of games and Ping-Pong paddles aren't worth it."

"We don't call our patients crazies," she corrected him. "If you'll follow me, I'll accompany you to the recreation room and then show you off the ward."

Cassidy heard them walk back toward the rec room. Thank goodness for Brian. When she was sure they were inside the room, she stepped out of the doorway and raced down the corridor in the opposite direction.

At the end of the hallway, a ward attendant spotted her. "What are you doing out there by yourself?"

"The nurse kept me late to talk to me. I'm coming back to my room."

The attendant glanced around. "Regulations are getting sloppier and sloppier around here. Soon we'll have locked-ward patients roaming freely all over the sanitarium." She opened the ward door for Cassidy. "Don't think you can get away with anything," the attendant warned. "I'm keeping an eye on you."

A little too late, thought Cassidy, and hurried to her room.

Late afternoon, and the sound of crying. Whose tears?

Cassidy listened to the voices of those in the rooms nearest hers. Through the walls of her room, she heard strident shouts and plaintive whimpers. The angry, and the lonely ones. She heard them, and wondered if Brian would take her message to Matt, and if Matt could find a way to get her out of here.

There was no social time before or after the evening meal, no chance to talk to Bill or Robin about what they'd seen while living in this place. Dinner was served in the rooms. Medicine was distributed with the food, and strictly supervised by the nursing staff.

"I don't need any pills." Cassidy was determined not to take any medicine Dr. Randall prescribed. She pushed the paper cup holding the two orange tablets away from her, across the tray.

"You'll have to take them you know," warned the nurse. She was younger than the ward supervisor. "They'll make you."

"I don't need any drugs; there's nothing wrong with me," said Cassidy.

"Dr. Randall thinks you need these. Come on, don't make a fuss. They can be rough if you don't do what they tell you. I don't want to see you get hurt. I'd take them if I were you."

Cassidy considered this. Her imagination didn't have to work overtime to conjure up a scene with orderlies holding her down and the nurse forcing her to swallow the tablets. It was easier to cooperate.

She poured the tablets into her hand. "Could I have some water to wash them down?"

The nurse handed her a paper cup full of water.

Cassidy stuck the pills in her mouth, wondering what they were, and drank the water. "Satisfied?"

The nurse smiled. "I'm glad you decided to make it easy on us both. I don't like to see my patients upset, honestly. It's better this way. Besides, I'm sure Dr. Randall knows what he's doing."

"Right," said Cassidy. She had to be careful not to lisp the word, or reveal that the tablets were pocketed at the back of her cheek.

"I'll see you at lights-out," said the nurse. "I know it must be scary, being alone here. I'll try to stay and talk for a little while when I come back later. Okay?" She wasn't so bad. Of all the staff, this one seemed the most human and caring.

Cassidy nodded, then listened as the door closed and was locked. She spit the pills into her hand. What kind of drug was Randall trying to give her? Something to make her act crazy, or knock her out?

She scanned the room, looking for a place to hide the tablets. It wasn't easy. This room wasn't designed for privacy, or for opportunity to conceal belongings. If the pills were found, she'd go through one of the episodes the nurse warned her about, and that wasn't something Cassidy wanted to experience. Finally, she put the tablets in the toe of her hospital slipper. It was the only place she could think of, and she was scared someone would come in and discover the pills in her hand.

Two nurses did come in during the next hour. They checked Cassidy's vital signs, asked her if she

SOMEONE'S WATCHING 161

was sleepy, and left without volunteering a single sentence of ordinary conversation.

They're not here to be your friends, Cassidy thought. *They're guards and watchers.*

She listened to the night sounds of the ward. Someone was refusing a bath, but it sounded as if she was losing the battle. Cassidy pulled the covers closer around her, huddled in the lonely space of fear and silence.

Another voice shouted, "Hold her, she bit me!" That was the head ward nurse; Cassidy recognized the harsh voice.

One for our side, she thought, and smiled.

After a few minutes, the voices faded and stilled. Soon, the only sounds Cassidy heard were the footsteps of the nursing staff going from room to room, the doors unlocking, and locking again. The enforced silence was worse than the sound of crying, worse than the angry shouts. The silence said she was alone.

A metal clink announced a key turning in the lock of her door. The young nurse peered through the opening. "Still awake?"

"I've been waiting for you." The truth was, Cassidy would have spoken to anyone, even Dr. Randall himself. She didn't want to be alone. Not tonight. Not here. "Can you come in?"

"All right, for a little while." The nurse sat on the end of Cassidy's bed. She didn't mention the chair that was missing from the room, although Cassidy was sure she'd heard about the incident.

"What's your name?" Cassidy asked.

"Beth. I'm new to this sanitarium, like you. I've only been here a month."

"How do you like it?"

Beth laughed softly. "Oh, they work us pretty hard, I guess. It's like anything else. You get used to it."

"I won't." She was being defiant. She knew she shouldn't have said it, as soon as the words were spoken.

"No, you won't, not if you're going to have that attitude," said Beth. "I don't think you understand. If you want to get along here, you'll have to cooperate. I've seen what happens to those who don't."

"I'm not crazy."

Beth got up to leave. "I'm not a doctor, but you seem all right to me. That's true."

"Will you help me?" Cassidy knew she sounded desperate. It was hard not to jump up, grab Beth by the arm, and plead with her. "Listen, if you could only let me talk to my parents . . . if I could use a phone . . . please, just for a few minutes."

Beth backed toward the door. "I couldn't do anything like that. I'd lose my job."

"You've got to help me. Dr. Randall's going to kill me. I know he will. He killed another woman in this sanitarium."

"What? What are you saying? Killed someone? Did you really take your medicine?"

"I—I took them." Cassidy tried to lie, but wasn't much good at it.

"You didn't, did you?" Beth opened the door.

"That was very foolish. I'm going to have to report it."

"No, please don't tell them."

"I warned you to cooperate. I tried to make it easier."

Beth closed the door and locked it from the outside.

"Don't tell them," Cassidy called to her. "I'll take the pills next time, I promise."

The jingling of metal keys on a ring was the end of the visit. The room had grown dark again, and overwhelming with the weight of quiet.

Don't let them come for me, Cassidy prayed, over and over.

Completely alone, she thought of her mother—Annie. Was it possible that her mother was watching? Could she help her?

"I'm afraid," Cassidy whispered . . . to the unseen ear, to the unseen spirit that connected her to another life. "Oh, Annie . . . Mama, I'm so afraid."

In the night, she dreamed.

The park was wide and green with damp grass. The swing moved back and forth, slowing with a gradual lessening of motion, until it was still. The child, wide-eyed and as quiet as the darkening day, waited for her mother to come and push the swing.

A squirrel ran from grass to tree, and birds settled in the branches of surrounding oaks and sycamores. It was the closing of the day. Light fading. Soon, it would be night. Her mother was crying.

As the child waited, watching this narrow image of her world, she heard dried leaves crackle beneath approaching footsteps. Someone was coming.

"Go away, John. Leave me alone."

The man stepped from the shadow into the circle of moonlight. She saw his arm raised high, and the silvery blade of the knife in his hand.

"Don't, no don't!" screamed Annie.

This time, Cassidy watched it all. She didn't let fear turn her away. She saw in the dream what the child had seen so long ago. Saw, and remembered.

Her mother's eyes were worse than the screams. There was terror in them . . . as the knife plunged into her neck and tore across her throat.

"Mama!" Cassidy cried.

Now the man looked. He looked right at her. She saw the scowling V-shape of his brows . . . above the dark-liquid eyes.

"Dr. Randall."

Cassidy opened her eyes, awake and back in the present. She was alone in the dark, in a room of the locked ward, a patient of Dr. Stewart Randall's—the man who had murdered her mother.

She knew it now, remembered everything. It wasn't John Terrell who'd stabbed her mother that night. It was Stewart Randall. She's seen his face . . . finally risked looking into the nightmare, and had seen it all. He was younger, thinner, but it was he. There wasn't any doubt in her mind.

Cassidy was sure of something else, too. *He knows I've remembered, or that I am remembering.* That was why he'd brought her here, to silence her forever.

Like he'd silenced Rebecca Finley.

She had to get out of here, before he saw the truth in her eyes—that she remembered it all. If he knew, really knew, he wouldn't let her live another day. There had to be a way to escape. She couldn't wait for Matt to save her. Not now.

She lay beneath the thin blanket, shivering with cold and fear. Soon, it would be morning and she would have to act. Dawn was only a few hours away. The dark couldn't terrify her forever. Alone, she waited for the first light of morning, and wondered: *How am I going to escape?*

Seventeen

Morning arrived with the thumping of a door. Cassidy heard the sound in her sleep, a heavy *thwump, thwump,* like an amplified heartbeat. When the heartbeat yelled, she opened her eyes and woke up.

"Let me out of here!" The voice was a man's, loud and angry. *Bang!* the wall shook with the impact of a body colliding against the door. "I want out of here; I want out now!"

Cassidy recognized the voice. It was Bill.

The sound of other voices clamored in the hallway, nurses, orderlies, and attendants. Cassidy heard them yelling to each other.

"Wait, don't open it yet."

"The doctor's coming."

"Let him handle this."

Which doctor? Cassidy tried not to be afraid for Bill, but she was. She couldn't help it. He sounded so desperate.

"Move out of the way." The voice was unmistakable. No one else sounded like Dr. Randall.

She tried to hear what else Dr. Randall said, but his words were drowned out by the constant thudding against the door. Why was Bill acting like this? Something had happened, she knew it. Or, something was going to happen. . . . The thought throbbed in her mind. *Bill, what are they planning to do to you?*

She heard the crash when the door was unlocked and pushed open. There was a lot of noise then, Bill yelling, orderlies shouting at him and at each other, and other patients shouting from their rooms.

"Leave him alone."

"Don't hurt him."

"Whassha matta, Bill? Issh all right." That had to be Robin.

There was a sudden quiet, and then Bill yelled in pain.

Cassidy was angry, fear leaving her for pure, unbridled hatred. She pounded on her door, too. "Stop it! If you hurt him, I'll tell everyone about you. About Rebecca Finley. About my mother."

It was a threat she immediately wished she could withdraw. But there it was, out in the open. She heard the struggle when they grabbed Bill. He was bigger than most of the orderlies Cassidy had seen, but he was only one man against so many. From the sound of it, people other than Bill were getting hurt.

Someone yelled, "Watch out! Grab his arm. Hold him, will you."

"No!" screamed Bill. "Get off me! Get—"

The silence that followed was loud with menace. Cassidy couldn't see or hear what was happening to her friend, but she knew it wasn't good. Was it because he'd told her about Mrs. Finley? Was that why they were taking him away, and keeping him locked up?

Inside, where it didn't show, she felt her flesh shrivel. What was happening to Bill . . . how long before it happened to her, too?

"Annie," she whispered into the caged silence of her room, "help me. Please, if it's possible, help me."

No one caused any trouble during breakfast. The food was put before them, and everyone ate without comment or complaint. Cassidy didn't care how it tasted. She put the sweaty eggs into her mouth without looking at them. She didn't try to talk to Robin—didn't want to get her in trouble—but couldn't help glancing at the empty chair near the end of the table. Bill's.

All through breakfast and the time in the recreation room, she wondered if Brian had given her message to Matt. If Matt knew, could he have done anything about it yet? Matt wouldn't doubt her. He would break into Randall's office if he had to, see the files on Mrs. Finley, and those on Cassidy, and find a way to get her out of here.

Could he do that? Maybe not, but she had to believe it was possible. She had to . . . or go crazy. She'd become exactly what they said she was, insane. Which was just what Dr. Randall wanted. He could lock her away permanently, and keep her quiet. He could kill her, just as he had killed Annie and Rebecca Finley. No one would ever know he was responsible.

Except Matt. He'd know. And Matt knew how to get things done.

Recreation time was over much too soon. Cassidy walked meekly with the other patients, back to the locked ward and her room. When the medication cart came, she accepted the two orange tablets without protest, pressing them to the back of her mouth as she had done the day before. She drank the offered water, and asked no questions of the nurse.

"How are you feeling today, Cassidy?" asked Beth, the same young nurse from the day before.

"Fine."

"You're comfortable? Feel like you're settling in?" There was an odd, questioning gaze in the woman's eyes.

"Yesh." She knew it the instant the lisp gave her away.

"What have you got in your mouth?" Beth grabbed Cassidy's jaw and tried to pry it open.

Cassidy shoved the woman's hand away, spit the tablets out, and threw them across the room. "I'm not taking any pills, and nothing else Dr. Randall gives me. I don't trust him. He kills people."

"Now, Cassidy, I know you're upset, but what you're saying doesn't make sense. I've been nice to you, haven't I? You like me?"

She grudgingly answered. "You've been all right."

"Do you think I'd work for someone who deliberately hurt people? Come on, now. Don't make a commotion about this. We've had enough trouble around here today."

"Where's Bill? What happened to him?"

"He's fine. Don't worry about him right now. It's you I'm concerned about. I don't want you to be scared or hurt, but you have to take your medicine. It's prescribed, doctor's orders. If you don't take it willingly . . ."

"Leave me alone! I want to go home. I want to see my parents. Why won't you let me talk to them?"

"Cassidy, stop shouting. You'll—"

The door opened and the ward nurse stepped into the room. "What's going on in here? I could hear her all the way down the hall. We can't have this kind of disturbance, nurse." She turned back to the hall and called, "Orderly! We need assistance in here."

"No, I can handle it," said Beth. "She's upset, but she'll be fine, really. Just let me talk to her for a while."

"We don't have time to coddle patients. You'll learn that after a few months here. Today's an excellent time to begin your instruction."

Two orderlies ran into the room. Cassidy knew she was in trouble. One had a straitjacket in his hand. His eyes were intense, in the harsh light they looked almost glittering, like those of a stalking animal.

"Don't hurt her," said Beth. Cassidy saw fear in her eyes, too.

"Easy does it," said the one approaching with the straitjacket. "Don't fight. It'll go much easier on you if—"

Cassidy made a rush for the open doorway. She pushed Beth to the ground and ran over her body. There wasn't time to think of where to go, or how to get away. Just run. That was all she could do.

She almost made it through the door. One of the orderlies grabbed her foot and pulled. She fell hard, slamming her face onto the floor with a jarring impact to the bones of her cheek.

"Drag her in here," said the ward nurse. "Get that straitjacket on her, and let's get on with this. I've had about enough trouble from willful patients for one day. First, that Bill. Now, this stubborn girl."

Cassidy's ankle was twisted and wrenched as the orderly dragged her back into her room. She cried out sharply, feeling as if her foot was being torn from her leg.

"Be careful," said Beth. "Don't hurt her."

"You're not helping your patient with this misplaced compassion, nurse," said the one in charge. "The sooner this procedure is finished, the better off she'll be."

The orderlies grappled with Cassidy, forcing her arms into the despised straitjacket, and securing the straps at the back.

"Why are you doing this!" Cassidy screamed. She was beyond control, now. She was scared, hurt, and outraged.

"It's for your own good," said the ward nurse.

"We don't like to force-feed or force-medicate our patients, but when it's necessary . . ."

Cassidy saw the long tube in the orderly's hand. "No!" she screamed, twisting her head and struggling . . . as the feeding tube was thrust into her mouth and down her throat.

"Hold her head," said the older nurse. "And bring me some water. Nurse!" she demanded of Beth, "bring me some water and those pills."

Beth brought the water and two more orange tablets. Cassidy tried to speak with her eyes, the only communication left to her, pleading with Beth, but the younger nurse handed the pills to the other woman. She didn't look into Cassidy's eyes—not now.

The pills were put into the paper cup of water, and poured into the feeding tube. Cassidy felt the mixture go down her throat, choking her. Like drowning. She struggled, trying to sit up, trying to cough, strangling.

"Let her up," said Beth. "That's enough, let her up!"

"All right, we're finished," said the ward nurse. "Remove the tube and let go of her."

It was horrible, horrible. The plastic tube being drawn out felt like part of her throat being skinned and ripped loose. She would have screamed, but couldn't. Instead, she was left gasping for breath and trembling with shock.

"That's how it's done," said the older nurse. "This is what happens when you coddle patients;

you make it worse for them. Do you understand, nurse?"

"Yes."

"Fine. I have other work that requires my time. You stay and finish up here. Get her into bed. You orderlies come with me. It's time to check on Bill."

The three left the room. Cassidy began to cry, hopeless sobs that poured from her like blood from a deep wound. The drug—whatever Randall had prescribed—was in her system. He was winning, and in spite of everything she'd tried to do to help herself, it didn't seem to matter. No one would help her. No one would save her from this place. Even her parents had abandoned her.

"Don't cry," said Beth, slipping a comforting arm around Cassidy's shoulders. "I'm sorry; I'm so sorry. It's over now."

But it wasn't over. Cassidy knew Dr. Randall wouldn't be satisfied until she was dead, unable to tell anyone what she knew about him. He had killed her mother, butchered her with a knife. A surgical scalpel—was that what he'd used? Now, he would kill the only witness to the murder, Cassidy.

The drug stole into her mind like thick fog, dulling her senses. Her vision blurred. Images shifted and remembered sounds and voices entered her thoughts from unexpected doors. It was as if the corridors of her mind had been subtly moved and new pathways emerged. Out of those pathways came nightmares.

She was younger, four or five. Her father was with her, holding her hand, taking her to school. Children everywhere, running, laughing, playing games. Cassidy wanted to play, too. She wanted to run like them, and chase the ball, and—

She saw the swing. Another girl was sitting on it, not swinging, only sitting still. Cassidy felt the chill of remembering that moment, a cold that ran through her veins, to her nerves, and into the new pathways of her mind. The little girl on the swing stared, not knowing the horror Cassidy was remembering . . . not understanding when Cassidy started screaming.

She felt the struggle within her now. The same screams. The same terror.

Her father had raced with her, away from the school and the playground. She remembered his arms around her, soothing her fear, trying to silence her screams. He carried her in his arms. Strong arms that protected her from any hurt. *Daddy. Where are you, Daddy?* He carried her into the glass and shining building . . . and into Dr. Randall's office.

No!

Cassidy saw the moment, as vividly as if it were happening this instant. The drug had opened the locked door to where this memory was stored. In her mind, she saw Dr. Randall as he was then. Younger. His hair darker. His eyes staring at her.

"Leave her with me, Burke. She's in a state of shock. I don't know what happened, but I'm concerned that this may lead to another episode of passive withdrawal from everything around her. I'll need to watch her for a few days."

Daddy, don't leave me. I'm scared.

But he did leave. He left, and she was alone with Dr. Randall.

"Cassidy, you remember me, don't you?"

No answer.

"You saw me that night, and you remember. Isn't that right?"

No answer. Look away from him. Look anywhere but at his eyes.

"Cassidy, look at me." He took her face in his hand. Turned it toward him and held it with hard-pressing fingers. "What are you afraid of?"

"School," she lied.

He took his hand away from her face. "You mean you're afraid to go to school?"

"It was scary. Teachers. Don't like it."

"That's all? Nothing else frightened you?" He physically moved back, the tenseness in his body visibly relaxing.

"I'm scared of the big kids." She knew, even at that age, he was listening to her words, believing her. And she knew, because of the lies, she was safe. Not long after this, her father came and took her home.

He would have killed me. She understood that now. She had saved herself once, instinct telling her what to do, but now it was too late. Randall knew the truth. He had her in her care, and there was no one to protect her from the doctor's *treatments*.

The images faded and Cassidy slept, fitful and restless, the drug weakening her strength, but not her spirit. Somehow, she would find a way to live.

Eighteen

"Wake up." The words were not softly spoken, but jarring and insistent.

Cassidy blinked her eyes, trying to dispel the double image of ward nurse Roberts.

"You've slept through lunch. That nurse took pity on you again, I expect. We'll have to do something about that later." The horror of the force-feeding tube flashed into Cassidy's consciousness. She was still wearing the straitjacket, her arms strapped to her chest.

"Ignorant woman," Nurse Roberts went on. "She's becoming more of a nuisance than the patients. I'll have to take over your care myself. For now, you have an appointment with Dr. Randall. Get up. I'll accompany you to his office. Can't trust anyone else to do things right."

The idea of Nurse Roberts taking over her care filled Cassidy with horror. At least Beth had some feelings. This other woman was inhuman, some kind of medical staff monster. Even Beth was to be taken away from her.

"Hurry up," demanded Nurse Roberts.

Cassidy felt the floor move beneath her feet

when she tried to stand. She was still woozy from whatever drug Dr. Randall had given her. It was difficult to stand and not fall over. Walking was even harder.

"Will you get on with it!" demanded the nurse. She yanked an edge of Cassidy's jacket and propelled her toward the door. The steel door seemed to spin, creating a wheel of shining metal in the field of Cassidy's vision. She felt herself falling into it, then was pushed through the now open doorway by the forward momentum of Nurse Roberts's arm.

"I'll fall," she cried. "Wait, I'll—"

A shove brought her into the hall, where a long line of doorways stretched into the vision of a shining, gap-toothed mouth. She tried not to look, not to see, but the tunnel grinned at her with menace that threatened like snapping teeth.

"I don't want an appointment with Dr. Randall. Don't make me go there. Don't make me."

"Stop this nonsense. You have no idea how busy Dr. Randall is—he's a very successful doctor—and he's making time in his busy schedule to see you. Of course you'll keep your appointment. It's obvious you need psychiatric help. You should be grateful that someone like Dr. Randall is there for you."

No argument would win against Nurse Roberts. Cassidy went where she was led, stumbling behind the woman, a corner of the staitjacket's sleeve gripped in the nurse's hand.

Dr. Randall's office door was locked, like all the

others in the psychiatric ward. The nurse produced a key from the ring at her belt. She opened the door and directed Cassidy inside. "Wait there," she told her, pointing to a plaid-patterned couch. "I'll tell Dr. Randall you're here."

She left Cassidy. The sound of the key turning in the lock was her goodbye.

I've got to get out of here. There wasn't much time. He would be there in a minute, and then it would be too late to save herself. Panic rose in her like the swift moving waters of a flood. He'd open the door, he'd be there and . . .

And then he was.

"Cassidy," he said, closing the door behind him, "so we finally come to this."

The room smelled sweet, an odor of lime or oranges—Dr. Randall's cologne. He pulled a chair in front of her and straddling it, sat directly opposite. He thoughtfully chewed at the corner of his upper lip.

"I'm disappointed with your behavior since you've been at Braitwithe. The nurse tells me you've tried to commit suicide."

"What! That's not true."

He sighed deeply. "I wish I could believe you; I really do. Miss Roberts is a reliable member of our nursing staff. She's been with me for many years. I must give heavy credence to her accusation. She says you've been hoarding your pills, in order to overdose."

"That's not why I did it."

"You admit you accumulated the pills?"

"No—well, yes. I didn't take them, but not because I wanted to kill myself."

"Two pills were found hidden in your bedroom slipper, and you were caught in the act trying to save another dose of two tablets this afternoon."

"I don't need any drugs."

"I brought you here to prevent your suicide, Cassidy. You're in a locked ward, because I'm afraid it's what might happen. If you could only realize we're trying to help you."

She wanted to shout—*Help me? You're trying to kill me*—but didn't. Didn't . . . because no one here would save her. She had to save herself. Or die.

The sudden movement of his hand startled her. He touched the fabric of the straitjacket. "I see the staff thought you would hurt yourself. They only do this for the patient's protection. Apparently, I'm not the only one who feels you might endanger your life."

She tried to think of something that would help her. "I guess I couldn't hurt myself now, could I? Or take an overdose? Not like this." If she were right about his planning to kill her with a lethal dose of drugs, then blame it on a suicide attempt, the straitjacket would be a problem.

He seemed to consider this. Clearly, it was a point he hadn't thought about. A change came over his face. It wasn't anger she saw, but recognition and realization. "You're a very bright girl. Just like your mother. Annie was clever, too. She knew about Mrs. Finley. She found Rebecca Finley's file in my office. Annie worked for me as my nurse. Did you know your mother was a nurse?"

Cassidy shook her head.

"No? Oh, yes. She was a good nurse, although a little too thorough. She did some research, and figured out what happened—that I had killed Mrs. Finley with an overdose of narcotics, and then blamed her death on drug-induced suicide. Arthur Finley collected his wife's estate, and we shared the inheritance as we'd planned. Annie knew that's where I got the money for my practice. She would have gone to the police Couldn't be paid off. That's why I killed her."

When Randall said these words, Cassidy knew her life was over. He would never have told her this confession if he planned to let her live.

"Now you know the truth," he said. "I was right; you did finally remember me from the night of your mother's murder, didn't you?"

She didn't dare answer.

"No matter. I didn't feel like waiting anymore, wondering if you would put it all together. You know it now." He stood and stepped back from the chair. "What shall we do about you?"

Cassidy couldn't be silent anymore. "I saw you kill her. I knew it was you, and I've told other people. If you kill me, they'll—"

"Other people?" He laughed. "You mean Bill? He won't be a problem. Bill will remain in isolation for as long as I say is necessary."

She was horrified by the thought of what Bill's life would become, because of his act of friendship toward her. She was afraid to mention anyone else, for fear of what Dr. Randall might do to them.

"No, you're wrong about anyone blaming me for your death. Your parents will say I tried everything to save you, even going as far as committing you to a sanitarium for observation. They trust me completely. I was, after all, such a good friend of your mother's. And the staff of the sanitarium will testify how I worked overtime trying to help you. This is Sunday, did you realize?"

She had lost track of the days. Since she'd been here, time had slowed into one long span, not accounted in days. Plus, the drugs he'd given her had dulled her mind.

"Still, you were right about the straitjacket. That would have been a serious mistake on my part. How could a young woman take an overdose of narcotics if her arms were tied into restraints? A little tricky, huh?" He smiled.

His smile filled her with cold dread. He was a murderer, smiling before the act. He enjoyed killing; she could see it in his eyes.

"I owe you thanks, really. You saved me from having to come up with a difficult explanation." He took a step toward her, then stopped. "No, it would be better if someone else saw you free of the jacket. Corroboration for me."

He moved to the door. "Orderly, come here. See that the straitjacket is removed from this young woman immediately. I'm not in the habit of having my patients manhandled and bullied in this way. And see that you're careful with her," he added.

"She's in a frail state of mind. Just remove the restraints, then wait outside the door. I'll be back in a minute."

Cassidy knew she wouldn't live beyond Randall's coming back into the room. He was getting the drugs to kill her.

The orderly was rough with unbuckling the straps of the straitjacket. She didn't complain or do anything to delay him. She wanted her arms free. It would be useless to try to convince this orderly that Dr. Randall was planning to kill her. He wouldn't believe anything she said. Why waste time? There was so little time left.

The orderly jerked the sleeves of the jacket off her arms in one hard tug. The material had been tight and hot. Pulling it free was like shucking a second skin.

"You sit there and behave." He took the jacket with him, and left, standing just outside the closed door.

Randall would be back any minute. Cassidy had to escape, but how? The office was part of Braitwithe Sanitarium, an older building with high ceilings and wide, spacious rooms. Randall's office had bars on the windows, eliminating the possibility of jumping.

Lamps were used in the office, instead of the building's antique light fixtures—the wiring being too expensive to change throughout the building. The heat and air-conditioning was channeled through a large air vent in the ceiling. There was nowhere to hide, no way to run. Unless . . .

Cassidy tilted back her head and stared at the air vent again. It was wide, large enough for her to climb into, designed so that service workers could crawl along the vent shaft and make repairs. The opening was in a recessed part of the ceiling, and covered with a metal grill. If she stood on Randall's desk . . .

There wasn't time to wonder if it would work. She heard footsteps heading down the hall, coming toward the room. Randall. She climbed to the desk top, pushed on the ceiling grill, and pulled herself up. There was only a moment to reset the grill before the door to the office opened and Dr. Randall stepped inside.

Cassidy held her breath. Every nerve in her body was firing energy. Every cell of her skin was fully aware of his presence. She felt the danger like a fire burning around and through her. She didn't make a sound or dare to move. She couldn't see him, but she could hear.

Dr. Randall walked around the room, his footsteps quiet and slow. "Are you hiding from me, Cassidy? Maybe under the desk? That won't do you any good. It's best to let it happen quickly. That way, you needn't be afraid too long."

She heard him come around the desk. He was standing just underneath her. If she moved her foot, coughed, or sneezed . . .

"You may as well come out, you know. It's only a matter of time before I find you. Don't make me angry. I warn you, this can be easy, or hard. Your decision. Come out now!"

If she had been hiding anywhere in the office, she might have done what he said, his voice was so commanding. And angry. She heard the controlled fury in it.

His footsteps were heavier now, quickly moving from point to point in the room. She heard furniture shoved across the floor, and the drapes yanked back from the window. "Dammit! Where is she?"

Cassidy was trembling. How long before he thought of the ceiling? How long before he found her in here? If she could crawl along the air vent to another room, maybe there'd be a chance to escape. To live.

"Orderly!" Randall shouted. "You incompetent idiot, you've let her get away." She heard his heavy gait cross the floor, the sound of the door being yanked open, and Randall shouting, "Where is she? I told you not to leave the door."

"I didn't leave. No, sir; I swear I didn't."

"It's obvious she's managed to slip past you. If she gets away . . ." Randall didn't finish the threat. Cassidy could well imagine the expression on his face: scowling V-shaped brows, eyes dark with fury, and small white teeth chewing in agitation on his upper lip. She knew; she'd seen this look before.

"I'll find her, sir. Don't worry. She can't have gone far."

"For your sake, you'd better hope you find her." He slammed the office door behind him. "Now get—"

Randall never finished the sentence. A sound stopped the words on his lips. Hidden in the narrow duct of the ceiling air vent, Cassidy heard it, too. The grill cover of the air vent, jarred loose by the slammed door, dropped onto the table in Randall's office.

In the rarified silence of an untaken breath, Cassidy heard the office door flung open with such a force that it banged against the wall. "Clever girl," said Randall, rushing from the doorway to the desk.

Go! Cassidy's mind screamed the thought. On hands and knees, she scrambled along the narrow metal cylinder.

"Find out where this duct leads," Randall shouted to the orderly, "and block the exit. If you screw up again, it'll mean your job."

"I'll get her, doc. Don't worry."

"Hurry up, man. Quickly, before she gets away from us."

Cassidy heard and felt it when Randall climbed into the air vent shaft with her. The entire air vent vibrated with the percussion of his knees hitting the metal pipe. The rhythm of it was a sound—a deadly drumming. Faster. Catching up. Faster.

Let there be an opening, she silently pleaded. *A way out. Anyplace away from him.*

She could hear noises in the rooms beneath the ceiling duct. Voices. The ducting system ran throughout the building, branching in several directions, some offshoots leading to vented openings like the one in Randall's office, and some leading to blank walls. Dead ends. She would be dead if she took one of these.

It was threateningly dark in the pipe, too dark to see how close Randall was behind her. Too dark to see anyone else coming toward her, either. If the orderly climbed into the air vent from somewhere up ahead, he could be crawling toward her right now. She could be trapped between the orderly and Randall.

Don't think of that. Keep moving.

A filtered play of light came from each grill opening Cassidy passed. At one of these, she turned and saw Randall. Only a few feet behind. His eyes, shining with murderous intent. In one hand was a filled syringe. *Deadly doses;* she knew.

A fork in the vent branching was up ahead. Which way? One might lead to life, the other to death. Right or left? She listened, and thought she heard voices on the right. Survival instinct led her toward them. *Help me. Please help me.*

She was running, on hands and knees she was running. Gasping for air. Terrified. Randall was the breath at her feet. He was the needle she would feel jabbed into her leg, and her last sight in life would be of this labyrinth tunnel.

Up ahead, would she see the grinning specter of the white-suited orderly? Or would she find escape through the fretted grillwork of an air vent? *Hurry. Hurry before—*

The vent grill up ahead allowed enough light for Cassidy to see to the end of the tunnel. Blank wall. No escape. No chance of turning around and going back. Randall was right behind her. No other choice than to pull off the grill and drop into the room. Now or never. *Do it.*

Lunging forward, she forced her fingers into the laced metal pattern of the grill cover and pulled. Nothing happened. Frantic, she pulled again. The grill was fixed in place, either nailed or bolted shut. It wouldn't move.

Cassidy turned and saw Randall . . . the syringe in his hand, needle point silvered in the fractured light. Like the knife that killed her mother.

"Mama!" she screamed, just as she had when she was the two-year-old watching the rise and fall of the man's arm, watching the knife, her cry echoing along the tunnel passage and into every room on the floor.

Like that night so long ago, he came at her.

Her back was pressed against the wall. She heard the drum of running, or was it the pounding of her heart? All her life blended into that one instant, that one flickering of light on a killer's face.

In the epiphany of a moment, Cassidy felt her mother's presence before her, shielding her in this dark tunnel, somewhere between the places of life and death. She felt the nearness of her mother's love. It surrounded her like a blanket of salvation. In the span of a single heartbeat, they were united again . . . as they had been once, as they would be always.

From the ceiling of the room below her, the metal grillwork covering the vent was kicked free. It clattered against the interior pipe. A hand reached into the square of sudden light, grabbed Cassidy by the leg, and dragged her out of the blocked tunnel.

John Terrell. She was pulled free, and fell into his arms. She had only a moment to see his face, the concern in his eyes, before he handed her to someone else.

"Matt!"

His arms went around her, drawing her to the side of the room and safety. "Cassidy," he said, holding her close. "When I got your message, I was so scared for you. Brian said you sounded desperate. Thank God you're all right."

She couldn't believe Matt was really here, or that the cop, John Terrell, was dragging a struggling Dr. Randall from the crawl space of the air vent.

"How did Terrell know about this?" she asked Matt.

"I told him. And he told me things—a lot of things—but we'll fill you in on that later."

Cassidy let all the questions wait. She watched John Terrell slam Dr. Randall against a wall, take the lethal syringe out of Randall's fingers, and handcuff him. "You move," he warned, "and I'll use whatever's in this on you."

Randall stopped struggling immediately.

It was like a dream, but she knew she really heard the words. "Stewart Randall, you're under arrest."

"For what?" Randall's eyes glared hatred at them all.

"For the attempted murder of Cassidy Thornton, and for the homicides of Anne Logan and Rebecca Finley."

The rest was a blur. Cassidy saw and heard it, but her attention was somewhere else. In that atoning moment, she was conscious only of her mother's spirit—at last set free.

Nineteen

"You're my father?" Cassidy asked.

"Yes," he said. "You're Annie's child, and mine."

John Terrell sat across from her at a quiet corner table of Beckham Place. The restaurant was a British-style prime rib and Yorkshire pudding kind of dinner house, with a crackling fire on the grate, and high-backed, overstuffed Queen Anne chairs at the tables.

This dinner together came a week after Stewart Randall was charged with Cassidy's kidnapping and attempted murder, and with the charges of first-degree homicide in the deaths of Anne Logan and Rebecca Finley. Randall was in jail, awaiting trial on all counts. From the looks of things, he would never set foot outside prison walls. The career he had been willing to jeopardize and destroy so many lives for was over.

Cassidy's nightmares were over, too. Now that the shadows were clear and she understood who had killed her mother, and why, the haunting dreams were gone. She had been freed of far more than the locked ward of Braitwithe Sanitarium. She had been freed of her terrible memories, too.

The reunion she had with her parents was strained by emotional pulls. Cassidy couldn't help feeling betrayed by their action, or inaction, of allowing Dr. Randall to commit her to Braitwithe against her will. That was hard for her to accept, and would take time to forgive. She loved them, knew they'd thought it was for her own good, but the memories of feeling abandoned would be part of her for a long while.

Seeing her mother in such frail health when she returned from the hospital brought a rush of loving feelings for both her parents back to Cassidy. No matter what they'd done, they were the ones who'd taken care of her all these years, the ones who'd loved and tried to do their best for her. Seeing her mother's face, the evidence of what the heart attack had cost her, and how close Cassidy had come to losing her, pushed all the bitterness away. In its place, there was only room for love.

After her parents learned what John Terrell had done, that he'd saved Cassidy from being killed, that he was not responsible for Annie's death, and that he'd caught and imprisoned the man who was, they encouraged him to become a part of Cassidy's life. They admitted they'd been wrong about him, and wanted to make up for lost time. This dinner was the first of many evenings Cassidy and her natural father would spend together, learning to know each other.

"Were you in love with my mother?" The question had no preface; what one could there be? It

SOMEONE'S WATCHING

was a subject that had troubled her, ever since she'd learned she was illegitimate.

He answered without pausing to think about it. "Annie and I loved each other very much."

"Then why..." She didn't know how to finish.

"Why didn't I marry her? Is that what's bothering you?"

"I guess. Especially after you found out she was going to have a baby."

"That's just it, I didn't find out about the pregnancy. Annie didn't tell me. I didn't know about you until two and a half years after your birth."

His answer amazed her. "But if you loved each other, why wouldn't she tell you?"

His deep sigh told her it was hard for him to answer. "We were young. Annie was only eighteen when you were born. I had planned on going to the Police Academy. We knew it would be hard for us, during the time I was in the academy and in training. Annie didn't want me to join the force. She was afraid for me, I guess. I suggested that we not see each other for a while."

He looked sad, too sad to go on with the story, but he did.

"Annie knew being a cop was what I wanted, so she didn't try to talk me out of it, and she didn't tell me about you. She knew that would have changed my mind. She kept her secret for the whole time I was in the academy and during the first few months of training. After you were born, she moved, and I lost track of her. She decided not to burden me with a child."

"Burden you?" Cassidy felt resentment against the word.

"That's how I felt when I heard it, too. I was angry that she'd kept you from me. Angry that I'd never known about my own daughter, and that Annie hadn't trusted me enough to know I would have given up everything to take care of her—if I'd known."

Cassidy remembered something. "Is that why you argued?"

"Argued?"

"I remember a day in the backyard of the house on Oak Knoll. You were standing in front of a bougainvillaea bush with Annie. I heard you arguing."

He looked surprised. "You remember that?"

"Yes, and someone taking my hand as we walked up the porch steps. He called me 'Button.' That was you, wasn't it?"

"I think I did call you Button. It's been so long, but I remember now. We argued that day over why she hadn't told me the truth. I was hurt and angry. If I hadn't left her the way I did, she might not have gone to the park that afternoon, and maybe . . ."

"It wasn't your fault." Cassidy knew this finally, and wanted him to know it, too. "My mother died because of Stewart Randall. He's responsible, no one else."

John Terrell reached into the pocket of his jacket. "Here, you'd better have this back." He handed her the DMV copy of Annie's license.

"How did you get this?"

"I took it from your room."

"You what?"

"I was worried when I figured out that you were searching into Annie's records. I knew her killer was still around. I was afraid he'd realize you were looking for him, so I broke into your house and searched your room to discover how much you knew, and what you'd done."

"Isn't that illegal?"

He smiled. "Are you going to arrest me? You have to remember, by then, I knew you were my daughter. I felt I had to protect you as much as I could."

When he put it that way, she guessed she could understand. In fact, she was glad to know he cared that much about her. "But why did you take the copy of her license?"

He glanced away, as if to hide the expression in his eyes from her, the hurt. "It was the only picture I had of her . . . of Annie. I wanted to keep it with me."

"You keep it," she told him. Cassidy couldn't help it, she started to cry.

"Come on, don't do that," he said, wiping away her tears with the linen napkin. "You and I, we're going to get to know each other. You have parents you love—I'd never try to change that—but I'd like it if we could be family, too. What do you say?"

There was so much to say. He had saved her life, he and Matt. And he was the man Annie had loved. It wasn't his fault things had worked out the way they had. If he wanted her to be his family, she wanted it, too.

"I say, next time, could we go someplace less fancy and have pizza for dinner? Or hamburgers?"

He laughed. "You know something? I like pizza and burgers better, too. Let's get out of here. I'll take you to Baskin-Robbins for an ice cream."

"Cone or sundae?"

"Whatever you want, kid. From now on, that's what I'm here for—whatever you want."

Cassidy felt the shadows lifting from her life. As she walked from the restaurant beside this man, she knew, at long last, everything was going to be all right.

The investigation into Braitwithe Sanitarium produced several changes in the administration of that facility. Cassidy's testimony was instrumental in the dismissal of Nurse Roberts from the staff. Charges were pending on her criminal collaboration with Dr. Randall in the cases of Rebecca Finley and several other patients.

The nurse known as Beth was allowed to stay on at Braitwithe, and because of Cassidy's and other patients' statements attesting to her kindness, was promoted to Nurse Roberts's position of ward supervisor.

Bill was a more difficult problem. Cassidy saw that he was released from isolation, where Dr. Randall had confined him. John Terrell made sure Bill was released from the locked ward, and released, if he wanted to be, from the sanitarium.

The problem was, Bill wasn't sure he did want to leave Braitwithe.

"I've been here for so long," he told Cassidy. "It's more my home now than anywhere else. And besides, people don't stare at me here the way they used to on the outside. People with problems of their own are more tolerant of others, I guess."

"Does that mean you want to stay at Braitwithe?" It sounded awful to her, but if it was what Bill wanted . . .

"I don't want them to force me to stay," he explained. "I'd want to be free to choose, but maybe I could work here, or something. It seems like home to me, and I care about so many of the patients. Do you think I could do that?"

She checked with administration. When Officer Terrell told them that Bill Martin might be willing not to bring charges against the facility for the many years of deprivation of his freedom, in exchange for gainful employment and a place to live at the sanitarium, they agreed immediately.

They also agreed to release Robin Sanders, with the added condition that the sanitarium would be responsible for Robin's medical and living expenses during the time needed for corrective surgery to repair her cleft palate, and a period of job training. Robin wanted to try life on the outside. Like Cassidy, she wanted to be free.

Prom night was wonderful. Cassidy and Matt danced beneath the twinkling lights of the hotel ballroom. The dresses were beautiful, the music great, and Matt was beside her in his pleated white shirt, turquoise cummerbund, and slate gray tuxedo.

They stepped outside the ballroom to the patio with its soft breeze and the brushed splendor of the night sky. The world had slowed, time encased in the quiet perfection of this moment. Even the stars were there for them, and no one else. That's how it felt.

They walked hand in hand to a private place, where no one could see or hear them. There, Matt leaned close and kissed her. She felt the drawing of love, from her to him, opening doors within her spirit that up until now had been sealed. It was freedom of another kind, and she wondered at the new, awakened feelings it brought. There was still so much to learn about life, and love. There was time. And there was Matt.

"To think, how much I almost lost," he said. His breath was warm against her cheek. "Someone was watching out for you."

She felt it, too. Someone was watching. Annie, her mother. Cassidy knew it now. When her life had been threatened, she'd felt Annie's presence protecting her, like a shield standing between Cassidy and danger.

That shield was gone now. Annie's spirit had been freed. Cassidy looked out among the glittering stars, like brilliant eyes on the face of night. Far away, but connected still. All through her life, Cassidy would feel the special bond of her mother's love, and know.

Someone was watching.

About the Author

Jessica Pierce lives with her family in La Cañada, California. She is also the author of SCREAM #3: WANTED TO RENT. Jessica loves to hear from her readers and you may write to her c/o Zebra Books, 475 Park Avenue South, New York, New York 10016. Please include a self-addressed stamped envelope if you wish a response.

DEADLY DETENTION
by Eric Weiner
(Coming Soon)

When it comes to punishment, no one dishes it out the way Harrison High's Mr. Crowley does. But there's something even weirder than usual going on today. No one knows that better than the six juniors and seniors who are being kept after school. The doors are padlocked. All the windows are covered with wire mesh. And the phone wires have been cut. No one can get in—or out.

And somewhere along the dark and deserted hallways of Harrison High, a sadistic madman lurks . . . waiting to administer his special brand of discipline.

The fatal kind . . .

Please turn the page for an exciting sneak preview of
DEADLY DETENTION!

One

It was quarter to four on a cold December afternoon.

Classroom #301 sat empty.

Waiting.

Then the door swung open sharply. A pretty seventeen-year-old girl stuck her head inside, her ice-blue eyes coolly surveying the room.

Like every other room at Harrison High, classroom #301 was groty and drab. Five rows of battered desk chairs faced the gray metal teacher's desk. A few posters decorated the walls, their edges curling. Dust motes danced dully in the beams of fading sunlight.

The girl turned and called back into the hall. "Glen? C'mon! We're the first ones."

She dumped her books on the arm of a desk chair in the front row. Sat down. Got up again. Normally, Jaclyn loved to sit in the front row, especially for classes with male teachers. Her short skirts drove them wild. But this was detention, she reminded herself. The less attention she got, the better.

Detention. Kids hated it even more than trips to

the principal's office. But Jaclyn wasn't feeling glum. She was feeling keyed up, excited. She'd never had detention before in her life.

She shifted to a seat in the middle of the second row. Her short-short, ultrabright vinyl skirt crinkled noisily each time she moved. "Glen!" she called again.

She had left the classroom door wide open. In walked a tall seventeen-year-old boy carrying a large pile of books under one arm. His handsome face was blank—and wary. He stayed near the door. "This is so ridiculous," he said. "I mean, I'm missing basketball practice for this."

Thanks to his grace in all athletic games and his almost movie-star good looks, Jaclyn's boyfriend was one of the most popular kids at Harrison High. As far as Jaclyn was concerned, though, he was also stupid. She stopped chewing her wad of gum and tilted her pretty little chin downward as she gave him a look of exaggerated surprise. "You're missing practice? Gee. What a great point, Glen. When the detention monitor arrives, why don't you just explain that to him?"

She reached inside her orange Varsity cheerleading jacket and pulled out two tiny earphones, which she slipped into her ears. With a toss of her head, she hid the earphones behind her hair. Then she pressed the sleeve of her jacket. There was a tiny click. Hidden inside the jacket's arm was an Aiwa Walkman, which she had just turned on. She started nodding her head back and forth to the music. She shut her eyes.

Sometimes, with guys like Glen, the best strategy was just to ignore them. . . .

She's ignoring me, Glen thought with disbelief. And the next thought was one that had been going through his head for weeks. Why was he still going out with her?

Jaclyn kept tossing her head to the music. She swayed sexily. She gave a little moan. Glen remembered why he was still going out with her.

He dropped his books on a desk and crossed to the window.

As signified by the number 3, classroom #301 was on the third and top floor of Harrison High. Still, the windows didn't afford much of a view. Last year all the windows at Harrison had been covered over with a thick wire mesh.

Glen really couldn't blame them for doing it. For years, kids had been sneaking over to the school grounds late at night and pelting the windows with rocks. Glen had done it himself, more than once.

Glen peered out through the grimy glass wire mesh. The sky was gray. Down below he could see part of the lawn; it was covered with slushy snow. He could also see the black macadam parking lot. There was plenty of activity going on down there. Kids were shouting to each other, slamming their car doors. They were so happy to be out of this place for another day. Glen sighed again, more deeply this time. There were butterflies in his stomach, like before a big game.

Still looking out the window, he muttered, "This place is like a prison."

"What?"

"I said—" Glen turned from the window, and remembering Jaclyn's Walkman, raised his voice several decibels. "I said this place is like a prison!"

Jaclyn clicked off her tape player. Then she crossed and uncrossed her legs. Her shimmery black tights made a swish sound that made Glen's heart thump. He couldn't help it. That swish sound excited him more than the swish he heard after taking a perfect shot in a basketball game.

Jaclyn said, "Come here."

Glen stared at her, his mouth slack. As he watched, she removed a large wad of green sugarless gum and stuck it under her desk. "I said come here."

"Why?"

"Why do you think?"

Glen didn't move. "What about this afternoon? I thought you said—"

"I told you to forget that."

Glen hesitated. "People will be here any second."

"No they won't." Jaclyn nodded up at the old wall clock. "We're early. We're the only fools who rushed to detention."

Shrugging his shoulders, Glen walked slowly down her row, slumping into the seat next to hers. When he put his books down, she took his hand. She held his fingers up to her face, sniffing them as if they were a bouquet of roses. Then she bit the tip of his forefinger so hard he yelped.

"Are you crazy?" he demanded.

"I wanted to get your attention."

"Well you got it!"

He tried to pull his hand away, but she held on to it. Smiling, her white teeth glistening, she now started to move his hand slowly down from her mouth. Down past the silver peace-sign medallion which hung around her neck on a thin black shoestring. Down past the open collar of her cheerleading jacket. Down.

Glen jerked his hand away. "Jaclyn," he said huskily. "C'mon, this is what got us into trouble in the first place."

"So?"

He shrugged. "So we gotta act like we learned our lesson, at least for one hour."

Jaclyn's ice-blue eyes looked even icier than usual. "You're a bore," she said.

"Jaclyn—"

But he didn't get any farther in pleading his case. Because just then Jill Berman, another senior, trudged into the room.

Jill was a tall girl with shoulder-length auburn hair that hung down limply around her head like something that had died. She had freckles and thick eyebrows that grew together a little bit behind her glasses. Her oily skin always had a slight sheen to it. And as if she wasn't burdened with enough problems, she was also fat.

What a sad case. Glen gave her his best smile. The truth was, he was glad to have the interruption.

Jill Berman stopped short as she entered the classroom. She was sure she was interrupting. It didn't seem right that the cheerleader and the basketball star would be in detention. "Oh, sorry," Jill said, peering at them through her thick glasses. "Uh . . . is this the right room?"

"Yup," Jaclyn said, studying her glossy red nails. "Overeaters Anonymous."

Jill laughed good-naturedly, her shoulders going up and down. She loved a good joke, even at her own expense. "You know, I actually do go to O.A.," she said. "Every Friday afternoon."

"No kidding," Jaclyn said.

"Yeah," Jill said. She smiled broadly. "I'm a card-carrying member. But isn't it funny they call it Overeaters *Anonymous?* Like no one knows I overeat, right?"

Guffawing at her own joke, Jill moved to the nearest chair and sat down, squeezing her legs under the arm of the desk. She grunted. It wasn't easy stuffing herself into the small space. They made such a fuss everywhere about making buildings accessible for handicapped people. They added ramps and elevators for people in wheelchairs. *You would think they would do something for fat people,* she thought bitterly. But no.

Turning in her seat—again with difficulty—Jill smiled at Jaclyn and Glen. Only Glen smiled back. There was an awkward silence.

Jill hated silence. She always felt compelled to fill it, just like she felt compelled to fill her stomach. "I've never had detention before," she said.

"Me neither," Jaclyn said, in a tone that seemed designed to end any farther discussion. The cheerleader turned away.

More silence. "I hope they serve snacks," Jill said.

Neither Jaclyn nor Glen answered. Jill looked at the large wall clock, then at her watch. She groaned. Her watch was fifteen minutes slow.

The watch, with its goofy Bart Simpson face and its pink leather band, had been a Christmas present from her mom, two years ago. Jill took it off her wrist and started carefully resetting the time. "This watch is always running slow," she said, "but I love it so much I can't bear to stop wearing it."

No one responded. There was tension in the room. Jill could feel it. She always felt tense waiting for a teacher. But this was worse. This was detention. Though Jill was trying to stay calm, or at least *look* calm, her stomach was already churning.

She studied Bart Simpson's yellow face. If only she could change time by setting the watch. She'd set it to five o'clock and this would all be over.

When she looked up, Glen was smiling at her, which made her feel a little better. "So what are you in for?" he asked.

"Child molestation," she answered. She giggled. "No, but seriously folks, Mrs. Howard caught me smoking in the bathroom. And speaking of cigarettes—God! I could really use one right now."

She opened her black drawstring bag and fumbled inside. She produced a jar of Stridex medicated buff pads, which she tossed back quickly, hoping Jaclyn and Glen hadn't seen. Fumbling some more, she pulled out two empty bags of Reese's Pieces and then a half-eaten jumbo bag of peanut M&Ms. She held the bag of candy toward Jaclyn and Glen. "Want one?"

Jaclyn disdainfully eyed the candy, arching one blond eyebrow. "No thanks."

Jill started popping two candies into her mouth at a time. "I'm so glad they started making the red ones again, aren't you guys? Even if they are carcinogenic."

"You shouldn't eat so much," Glen said, but he didn't say it meanly.

"You're right," agreed Jill. "The thing is, I'm really nervous about all this weight I've been gaining"—she popped another candy into her mouth and chewed noisily—"and junk food is the only thing that calms me down."

"Better be careful, Jill," said a voice at the door. "The green ones make you horny as hell."

"Mike Morricone!" exclaimed Jill gleefully. "Fancy meeting you here."

The junior strolling into the classroom was on the stocky side, with the powerful arms you might expect from a wrestler, which he was. He wore a purple Harrison High T-shirt, tight because of his many muscles, and a backward white cap. He was smiling his usual twinkly-eyed closemouthed smile.

He stopped at Jill's desk. "So you got detention, too? High-five!"

They high-fived loudly. *All right*, Jill was thinking, *Mike Morricone!* Things were looking up. Mike was Jill's definition of a fun-loving guy. The guy never had a care on his mind.

Trying not to grit his teeth or show how upset he was, Mike swung into a seat right behind the heavy girl's. He couldn't even look in Jaclyn's direction. He just nodded at the other two students—"Glen, Jaclyn." Then, smiling more broadly, he reached over to pat Jill affectionately on the back. "So, Berman, whadja do this time?"

"Oh, right, like I usually get detention," Jill said, laughing. She reached under her sweater and produced a pack of Virginia Slims, which she held up by way of explanation.

Mike's eyes went wide with surprise. "Since when do you smoke?"

"Since I started doing my college applications."

Mike laughed. But what he was thinking was how sorry he felt for her. The heavy girl was looking even more nervous—and fat—than usual. And now she was smoking. "You ought to relax, Berman," he told her. "Believe me—you don't have to worry about getting into a good school."

"That's what you say. I'm so wired I can barely sleep at night."

"Look, what difference does it make, anyway?" he asked, grinning. "That's what you have to ask yourself. School, college, grades—what's the difference? It's all a big joke."

"Some joke," Jill said.

"Here," Mike said, taking the cigarettes, "I'll help you quit."

She grabbed for the pack. "No way."

Mike laughed. "Just teasin' ya." He two-fingered a cigarette from the pack and slipped it behind his ear, then handed the rest back.

"What about you? How'd you get detention?" Jill asked him. "Wait a minute. Don't tell me. Let me guess. You farted really loudly in homeroom?"

Mike smiled proudly. His farting abilities were legendary at Harrison. As well they should be. He had once ripped off a doozy in assembly, right in the middle of a speech by Harrison's mayor, Mr. Hartley.

Mr. Hartley had been droning on for twenty minutes about the importance of scholarship. Harrison wasn't a rich town, said Hartley. Not like some of those fancy-pants Bergen County towns that were closer to Manhattan, such as Englewood and Montclair. No, said Hartley, Harrison wasn't rich at all. *But*—he waved a finger in the air—Harrison High was still famous. Famous for the quality of its teachers and famous for its long tradition of academic excellence. Why, for years the students of Harrison had proven that money wasn't everything. With diligence and hard work—

And right then Mike had farted so long and so loudly that he got detention for a week. Worth every minute, too.

"Nope," Mike now told Jill. "Didn't fart. Guess again."

"Okay." Jill thought a moment. "You made fun of Mrs. Walker!"

Mrs. Walker was the school nurse. She walked ramrod straight, and Mike loved to walk right behind her in the hallways, imitating her perfectly.

"Nope," Mike said. "It wasn't Mrs. Walker this time." He leaned back, two hands behind his head. "This time it wasn't my fault at all. My car wouldn't start. I didn't get here until after third period."

Jill cackled. "Right."

"I know, sounds like a dumb excuse, right?"

"Right," agreed Jaclyn, clicking her Walkman back on.

Ignoring Jaclyn's comment, Mike sat up, his arms spread wide. "Jill, I swear to God, that's what happened. Wake up this morning, the car is dead. Turn the key. Nothing. I don't mean, you know, a little sound like someday it might turn over. Silence. Not even a click."

"Maybe it's the weather," Glen offered.

"Right," Mike said curtly. " 'Course," he continued to Jill, "I wasn't too broken up about it. When I found out it wouldn't start, I called Triple-A and went right back to bed. I figured it's like a snow day. I was going to watch the game shows all day."

"All right!" exclaimed Jill. Then she frowned. "So what are you doing here?"

"Triple-A shows up at eleven, right before "Wheel of Fortune." All I got to see was cartoons. *And* I got detention."

Mike turned to the dirty-blond cheerleader a few seats away. He waited until she turned the tape back off, then asked, "Since when do they punish Miss Popular?"

Jaclyn made a face and tossed her perfect head of hair, as if to say, "Funny." What she really said was, "Miss Johnson caught us in the music room at lunch. Doing you know what."

Mike grinned, but humorlessly. He knew what.

"Why do you have to tell everybody about it?" Glen asked sullenly.

Jaclyn's head jerked in her boyfriend's direction. "Why? You ashamed?"

"No," Glen said quickly. "It's just"—he looked away. In a lower voice, he finished lamely, "I don't see why you have to tell everybody."

Jaclyn shook her head. "I don't like the way you're acting, you know that?" She pressed her sleeve and clicked her Walkman on again, disappearing rapidly into the music. She lolled her perfect head back, made little fists over her head and stretched kittenishly. She closed her eyes. And then she ran her pink tongue around her lips, moistening them slowly, so slowly.

Mike, who was still watching her, winced and said, "Ouch!"

This is going to be hell, he told himself. He turned back to Jill. "So who's covering detention today?"

"Well," Jill said, looking around the dingy classroom. "This is usually Mr. Osmond's room. So I'm praying it's him."

With his white hair and bony body, Mr. Osmond

looked like he was about eighty years old. He was not too strong on discipline, as you could tell by the amount of graffiti scrawled on the desks. In places where kids had pushed their desks up to the sides of the room, there was even graffiti on the walls. Mike himself had added his fair share over the years.

He placed his hands together in fake prayer. "Please, God, let it be Osmond, let it be Osmond."

Glen said, "Osmond was out sick today."

"Thanks a lot, God," said Mike.

"Just as long as it's not Crowley," said Jaclyn, who had turned off her Walkman yet again.

At the sound of Crowley's name, Mike's stomach—which was already tense—tensed up even more. Apparently the name had the same magical effect on all the students. All heads turned toward the cheerleader.

"Why would it be Crowley?" Glen asked, nervously running his hand through his short brown hair.

Jaclyn said, "It just could be, that's all."

"She's right. They rotate detention duty," Mike said.

"Thank you, detention expert," Jaclyn told Mike. Her voice was sugary with sarcasm. To Glen and Jill, she said, "The list is posted in the principal's office. I was in there today but I didn't see whether today is Crowley day or not."

"Oh, my God," said Jill. "Perish the thought." She started popping three M&Ms at a time.

"The Corporal for detention?" Glen said, shaking his head. He chuckled. "Hey—that'd be Corporal punishment."

No one laughed. For a moment, everyone in the room sat silently. The Corporal, thought Mike. He shuddered.

Mr. Lance Crowley (or "The Corporal," as students called him behind his back) was Harrison's biology teacher. Among parents and teachers, he had built up a reputation for being a tough but superb educator. Last year he'd even been written up in *The Bergen Record*. The article had talked about Crowley's boot-camp approach to education and science, but it had made it all sound like a joke, like something the students thought was fun. The article also pointed out that Crowley's science club had produced two Westinghouse scholars. The article said he was beloved by parents and students alike.

Well, the newspaper story got it half-right, thought Mike. The parents *did* love Crowley. The students—well, the students were a different story. The students had always been petrified. And the last couple of months . . .

"The guy was always strict," Glen said, "but lately . . . Sheesh!"

"I think the man is really flipping out," Jill agreed. "You should have heard him in class today. Betsy Doyle refused to pith her frog? Said it was cruelty to animals? So Crowley starts screaming at her. I mean, screaming his head off. He got his face right into hers, too, you know the way he does. Like a drill sergeant."

"Drill *Corporal*," Mike corrected.

"He was in the Marines," Glen said.

"Duh," said Jaclyn. Putting a hand up to the side of her mouth in a fake attempt at secrecy, she added, "He's got a drinking problem."

"Tell me about it," said Jill. "It's gotten so I can smell it from three rows back."

Jaclyn frowned at Jill, then said, "You know about the dart board?" Jill shook her head, wide-eyed. "He's got this dart board in the teacher's lounge. And he cuts out pictures from the yearbook of kids he doesn't like? And he tapes them right over the bull's-eye."

"That's a lie," Mike said. He tried to say it casually, to make sure Jaclyn didn't think he was scared.

"I swear." Jaclyn leaned forward, beckoning Mike and Jill toward her with the crook of a pretty finger. She lowered her voice to a stage whisper. "Get this. Crowley's son is like this total druggie."

"Oh, everyone knows that," Jill said matter-of-factly. "His son's been arrested twice for possession."

"I know," Jaclyn continued smoothly, "but did you know—" She paused for dramatic effect.

"Know what?" Glen asked.

Jaclyn grinned. "His wife is so upset about their son that . . . she's had this complete nervous breakdown thing where she's like afraid to go out of the house."

"No! Where did you hear that?" Jill asked, her jaw dropping.

"It's bull," Mike said.

"How do you know?" Jaclyn asked. Her blue eyes flashed.

Mike shrugged. "How do *you* know, that's the question."

Jaclyn curled her upper lip in a sneer. "My mother used to play doubles with Mrs. Crowley, okay? Last summer Mrs. C dropped out of the game and wouldn't give a reason. And when my mom finally spoke to Mr. Crowley about it, all he would say was that she *wasn't well*. Then she found out the true story from one of his neighbors, who she plays bridge with. Mrs. C had a nervous breakdown, I'm telling you."

The four students sat in silence a moment. "Well, it's not too surprising," Jill said at last. *"I'd* have a nervous breakdown if I was married to the guy."

"And I'd do drugs if I was his son," added Mike. "Hey, I do them anyway!"

Jaclyn bit off the cap of her black Bic. Pressing down hard, she started scrawling the pen back and forth on her desktop, darkening an already heavily inked groove in the wood. She kept her head down. "It's all because of the son," she said. "It's because of the son doing drugs that the mother broke down. Because she's so disappointed in him. And my mom says that's why Crowley's been so mean to all his students lately. It's because of what his son did. Now Crowley hates *all* kids. It's like he wants . . . revenge."

"Wow," Jill said. "That's awful."

They were all silent, listening to the clock tick.

Then the old radiators started their eerie knocking.

"You don't think we're going to get Crowley, do you?" Jill asked.

No one answered.

Tick, tick, tick . . .

"Now I'm really getting nervous," Jill said. "Somebody tell me I shouldn't be nervous, okay? Guys?"

"I don't know," Glen said softly. "If you ask me, the guy's really about to snap. He's like right on the edge. I was in the class the day he broke that pointer. I really thought he was going to go berserk and start stabbing everyone."

"Okay," Jill said. "That's enough. I'm starting to freak."

"Don't make me keep you after school," Jaclyn said, lowering her voice in imitation of Crowley's deep-throated rasp. "Don't make me do it. Because if *you* have to stay late, then *I* have to stay late. And that makes me *mad!*"

Jill gasped, and then laughed and applauded. So did Mike. Just about everyone at Harrison did an imitation of Crowley these days. But Mike had to admit it, Jaclyn's was one of the best.

Jill leaned back in her chair and tapped Mike's powerful shoulder. "Do yours," she begged.

Mike smiled, his eyes crinkling. He was tempted, but—He glanced toward the door. "I better not."

"Aw, go on," Jaclyn said. "You've already got detention. What's the worst that can happen to you?"

Mike thought for a moment. The last thing he wanted was to look like a coward in front of Jaclyn. On the other hand, he'd really be asking for it. He pushed himself up out of the chair. "Okay."

He immediately changed his posture, pushing out his stomach to imitate Crowley's barrel chest and swinging his arms as he walked in the biology teacher's bullying and apelike manner. He jutted his jaw forward, looking furious. He darted his head from side to side, as if trying to catch the other three students goofing off.

Then he walked behind the teacher's desk and mimed hoisting a heavy briefcase. He slammed both hands down on the metal desk top, hard, to imitate the way Crowley always dropped his briefcase. "Good morning," he barked. He made a little tsk sound, sucking on a tooth.

Everyone applauded. Mike grinned. He knew he had caught Crowley's mannerisms perfectly.

Jill whistled. He spun sharply, pointing right at her, his eyes dark with fury. "You making fun of me, Berman?"

Jill was laughing so hard now there were tears in her eyes. She forced out a "No."

"Don't make me keep you after school," he warned. "Because if you have to stay late, that means that I—"

"MORRICONE!"

The shout came from just outside the open doorway.

Everyone in the room jumped.

All blood drained instantly out of Mike's face.

Crowley!

"You *dare* to imitate *me?!*" Crowley shouted. "I'll *kill* you. You hear me? I'll kill you!"

Look for DEADLY DETENTION on sale at bookstores everywhere soon!

MAKE THE ROMANCE CONNECTION

Z-TALK
Online

Come talk to your favorite authors and get the inside scoop on everything that's going on in the world of romance publishing, from the only online service that's designed exclusively for the publishing industry.

With Z-Talk Online Information Service, the most innovative and exciting computer bulletin board around, you can:

- ♥ CHAT "LIVE" WITH AUTHORS, FELLOW ROMANCE READERS, AND OTHER MEMBERS OF THE ROMANCE PUBLISHING COMMUNITY.
- ♥ FIND OUT ABOUT UPCOMING TITLES BEFORE THEY'RE RELEASED.
- ♥ DOWNLOAD THOUSANDS OF FILES AND GAMES.
- ♥ READ REVIEWS OF ROMANCE TITLES.
- ♥ HAVE UNLIMITED USE OF E-MAIL.
- ♥ POST MESSAGES ON OUR DOZENS OF TOPIC BOARDS.

All it takes is a computer and a modem to get online with Z-Talk. Set your modem to 8/N/1, and dial 212-545-1120. If you need help, call the System Operator, at 212-889-2299, ext. 260. There's a two week free trial period. After that, annual membership is only $ 60.00.

See you online!

KENSINGTON PUBLISHING CORP.